David Hill

Placer gold or how Uncle Nathan los his farm

A New England drama in three acts by David Hill

David Hill

Placer gold or how Uncle Nathan los his farm
A New England drama in three acts by David Hill

ISBN/EAN: 9783743377356

Manufactured in Europe, USA, Canada, Australia, Japa

Cover: Foto ©Andreas Hilbeck / pixelio.de

Manufactured and distributed by brebook publishing software
(www.brebook.com)

David Hill

Placer gold or how Uncle Nathan los his farm

PLACER GOLD

OR

HOW UNCLE NATHAN LOST HIS FARM

A New England Drama in Three Acts

BY

DAVID

AUTHOR OF "FORCED TO THE ~~~~~~~~~ AN OATH"
"OUT OF HIS S~~~~

BOS~~~

18~

CHARACTERS.

NATHAN BARDWELL	*A farmer*
QUINCY BARDWELL } NED BARDWELL }	*His sons*
JAMES MONROE	*Chum to Ned*
JOSEPH MURPHY	*Bardwell's hired man*
SQUIRE CROSBY	*A miserly farmer with land joining Bardwell's*
MIKE O'CONNOR	*Crosby's hired man*
CHARLES MAYHEW } RICHARD BLYNN }	*Gold-mine swindlers*
SHERIFF	
MARIA BARDWELL	*Nathan Bardwell's wife*
BELLE BARDWELL	*The orphan*
NELLIE CROSBY	*Crosby's daughter*
MATILDA	*Crosby's hired girl, afterwards wife to O'Connor*
GIPSY	*The waif, living at Squire Crosby's*

PROPERTIES.

ACT I.

SCENE 1. — Ropes for jumping, basket, cake knife, money, bottle, silver knives and forks, doll, wreath of flowers, and necklace.

SCENE 2. — Fiddle, horns, drum, tin pans, etc. Blunderbuss and nightcap for Nathan. Bundle for Ned. Moonlight.

ACT II.

SCENE 1. — Bottle containing samples of ore. Documents for Crosby. Drinking-cup at well.

SCENE 2. — Hollow log to crawl into. Pick axes, shovels, axe, and pans for washing gold. Ore and gravel on stage. Stuffed owl. Two revolvers. Documents for Crosby, and pen for signing paper. Gold bricks. Small tin trunk for Gipsy.

ACT III.

SCENE 1. — Pipe for Joe. Bucket of water at well. Pistol for Gipsy. Gun and cane for Nathan.

SCENE 2. — Album on table. Package of money, Bible, and documents.

SCENE 3. — Torch for lighting. Large frame motto, "Welcome Home," for illuminating.

NOTE. — The elaborate scenery called for by this piece is only necessary in professional stage performances. For amateur production it may be much simplified, three scenes being all that are absolutely needed for full representation of the piece.

SYNOPSIS.

ACT. I.

SCENE I. — The bridal party on the lawn. **Ned Bardwell,** the runa-way. Uncle Nathan and Squire Crosby. " **The jinin' of** your darter ter my son has sealed a bond o' friendship atween us that ought ter last a lifetime." Mike O'Connor and his new clothes. Why he was two hours late. Fun by the bushel. Rope-jumping, song-singing and dancing. Distributing the wedding gifts. Joe Murphy left out in the cold. All promenade.

SCENE II. — Uncle Nathan's dooryard. The midnight serenade. Waking the married couple. Fiddle, horns and tin pans. The blun-derbuss. " Hello ! you, there ! ain't you hit ? " " Be jabers, I am; but the fiddle ain't." Welcoming the serenaders. Ned, the runaway. Picture in the window. " Ah, l could tell that face among a thous-and." His interview with Gipsy. A sudden farewell. Uncle Nathan excited. The serenaders happy. " Now that we've rousted the new bride, and feasted, and emptied the ould gintleman's cider jug, I feel loike taking my quiet departure." Act closes with song-singing and " Virginia Reel."

ACT II.

SCENE I.—Uncle Nathan's dooryard same as in Act I., Scene II. After eleven years. Time — morning. Nathan's story to Belle about the giant. " Was you always good, grandpa ? " Mike O'Connor creates a surprise. Crosby and the bogus mine swindler. They interview Uncle Nathan. Placer gold. Crosby's proposition. Nathan cautious. " Dog gone it ! how do I know there is any gold ? " The bogus offer and refusal. Plan to meet in Rocky Run Two documents and what they contained. Gipsy's warning. " If money cannot purchase your farm ; if you love it to the extent that your words imply, don't you sign those papers." Picture.

SCENE II. — The gold mine of Rocky Run. Mike and Joe digging for gold. Afraid of ghosts. Story of Tom Piper and the goose. Frightened by an owl. Almost discovered. A hollow log and a tree a place of security. Stealing information. Plot to rob Uncle Nathan of his farm. Caught listening. A peculiar predicament. Silenced for two hundred dollars. Crosby, Uncle Nathan and Belle. Placer gold in abundance. Uncle Nathan convinced of his good luck. Mort-gage on the farm. Gold bricks. A curious tablet " Here — here is my tablet, Crosby. It shall be innocence beneath these papers, an' a God ter witness 'em above, an' if evil is in 'em, may they burn the hearts of those who wrought 'em." The spectre among the rocks. Gipsy and the tin trunk. " Nathan Bardwell ! this is the gold mine of Rocky Run." A startling finale. Tableau.

3

ACT III.

SCENE I. — Uncle Nathan's dooryard as in Act I. and Act II. Without a home. Mike and Joe. They exchange secrets. Matilda again. Mike hides in the well. Overhears his wife making love to Joe. "Yeez can have her, Joe, yeez can have her." Discovered. A good ducking. Gipsy to the rescue. Last day at the old farm. Ejected by the sheriff. Gipsy and the pistol. "Lay a finger upon me, and you will find me a human tigress." Uncle Nathan protects his home. He is overpowered. Gipsy interferes. "Back! I say! Your authority relates to the farm and not to Nathan. Touch him again if you dare." Picture.

SCENE II. — Parlor in Crosby's house. Blynn in search of his daughter. His interview with Gipsy. The mysterious letter in India ink. Gipsy his long lost daughter. Refusing his caresses. "Wait! thankful though I am to find a father, etc." Blynn tells of his reformation. Ned Bardwell and Gipsy. Business first and love afterwards. The demand of Richard Blynn. Crosby's refusal. The two Irishmen. "We've turned state's evidence, your honor." Ned Bardwell's threat. Blynn's advice. Squire Crosby without a friend. Alone with Gipsy and Belle. The family Bible, and what it contained. Past memories revived. Melted to tears. "I thought I was hardened — case hardened; but I am not. There is a tender spot left yet." Never too late to reform. Sequel to placer gold. End of the mortgage. The way Belle disposed of a fraud. Picture.

SCENE III. — Uncle Nathan's dooryard as in other Acts. Back on the old farm. Time — evening. Curious conundrums. A poor man's experience. Has to dig through six feet of solid silver in order to strike gold. An old man's whim. Carries a twenty-pound weight five miles to balance a twenty pound weight on his way back. Matilda not to be outwitted. Visiting the old home. "Here we are, Maria, creepin' up ter our old home like two thieves in the night." He is shocked by hearing laughter within the house. "Did ye hear that, Maria Did ye hear that?" Not to be reconciled. "They have no hearts, no feelin's, no sense of compassion an' I'll tell 'em of it." Gipsy's welcome. Uncle Nathan in doubt. A grand explanation. Blynn and Crosby give back the farm and crave forgiveness. Two grandpas to love now. A second surprise. Ned in the arms of his parents. Too happy for utterance. "Maria, I — I'm young again. I'm put back twenty years in life." The illuminated motto, "Welcome Home." A happy termination.

PLACER GOLD.

ACT I.

SCENE I. — *A lawn interspersed with trees, vases of flowers, etc. Landscape back to match. An ornamental fence running across stage back with archway in center. Set trees* L. *and* R. *Symphony of chorus in the distance as curtain rises. Enter,* C., *two young girls dressed in white, each holding a wand. They remain standing each side of archway. These are followed by* QUINCY *and his bride, the young people,* SQUIRE CROSBY *and* MATILDA, *and* UNCLE NATHAN *and* MARIA. *They all form two lines toward front. The two in white now pass down center and around the outside, followed by the others in order as in a promenade. After circling twice or more around the stage, the two in white pause* L. I E., *one on each side of entrance, the others pass through, and are followed by the two in white. For effect there must be no pause, and singing must be continued until all have disappeared.*

SONG.

AIR. — "*Come merry birds in winter.*"

Wake ! merry hearts, awaken !
Make the bright welkin ring,
Loud with our shouts of gladness,
Vocal with songs we sing.
Cheerful and happy ever,
Free from all sorrow and pain,
Shout ! for a day so joyous
To us will not come again.

Chorus. — Oh, we will scatter flowers
Along the smooth highway,
This ever bright and joyous,
Eventful wedding day.

Wake ! merry hearts, awaken !
Sweet wedding bells have rung ;
Two hearts are now united,
And beating same as one.
Cheer them along their pathway,
Sing them some happy refrain,
Shout ! for a day so joyous
To them, will not come again.

Chorus. — Oh, we will scatter flowers, etc.

(*All exeunt*, L. 3 E.)

(*Enter* NED BARDWELL, C. *He crosses to* L. 3 E., *and watches the party in the distance.*)

NED. There they go, chattering and singing like a flock of crazy blackbirds. Scattering themselves among the trees to feast on wedding sweetmeats, and stare at Quincy's bride. Ha! ha! ha! Quincy married, and I, his brother, turned out of the house. Well, I'm the black sheep among the flock — the bad egg out of the thirteen. I'm the governor's scape-goat. Didn't he say to me this morning, "Ned, quit this house; and don't you return until you can do so an obedient and dutiful son." (*Enter from* C., JOE *and* GIPSY *in great haste, and cross* L. *They are busily talking, and do not perceive* NED *in front of them.*) Haven't I left? Haven't I sworn never to return? I never will — (JOE *and* GIPSY *run against him.*)

GIPSY (*starting back in surprise*). O my!

JOE (*holding on to his head*). I'm struck wid a brickbat.

NED. Well, what do you take me for — the highway?

GIPSY. Oh, Ned! you are real mean.

JOE. Be jabers! he's a perfect jackass.

NED (*laughing*). That's what the governor said this morning. Complimentary, wasn't he? But I say, Gip, why aren't you with the rest?

GIPSY. What a question! Didn't I wait for you until I nearly missed the wedding? Didn't I wait for you at the church until all had gone, and Joe had to serve as my escort? Then didn't I get my dress caught on a brier? O Ned! I forgot. How do you like my dress? (*Whirling around.*) Pretty, isn't it? You ought to have heard the Squire groan when he paid for it. Why, he actually shed tears. But you haven't told me how I look?

NED. You haven't given me time. One would almost take you for the bride.

GIPSY. I wish I was. There! I don't either: O dear! what made you quarrel with your father? Then to disappoint me so. How could you?

NED. Well, Gip, it is unnecessary for me to explain. I may be to blame, I admit that; but I am too stubborn to return. I am going away.

GIPSY (*in surprise*). Going away, Ned?

NED. Yes — off to the mines. I'm going to strike gold or bust.

GIPSY. Oh, Ned, please "bust" just as quick as you can. Come! be reasonable. Here! I want you as my escort.

JOE. He-e-e-em.

GIPSY. Ha! ha! ha! — I forgot. You are my escort, aren't you, Joe? Well, we won't quarrel; but if he should consent —

JOE. Sure, thin I should be loike the ten vargins; left out in the cold.

NED. No, Gip. Go in as you have started; but when an opportunity offers, slip out and see me alone. I will hide among the trees until you return.

GIPSY. Well, just as you say. I have a good mind not to, though. It would serve you just right. Come, Joe. (*Wheeling him into line.*) Right about face — eyes to the front — steady — forward — march! (*They exeunt* L. 3 E.)

NED. What a girl. Full of life and spirit as the birds of the air. Gushing, at times, with laughter, then sentimental, then fierce as a mountain lion, with a temper that knows no bounds. Would that I knew the history of her birth.

MONROE (*enters* C.). Hello, Ned, repenting at leisure? Why, I'm all ready for a start.

NED. I shall be with you to-night. When darkness sets in, I shall enter my room by the window, secure my wearing apparel, and then farewell to home and friends.

MONROE. And to Gipsy at the same time. By Jove! I should hate to leave that piece of property behind. She's a claim by herself.

NED. Yes, and she may prove a lost claim to me. However, it is too late to repent now.

MONROE. By the way, Ned, how will the old man take it when he finds out you mean business?

NED. Oh, he looks at grief with a smile, and always did. My regrets are for my mother. A mother can never forget.

MONROE. Well, when we strike that hundred thousand, you can write home, and all will be forgiven. I tell you — you might repent now; ask the old man's forgiveness, marry Gip, and —

NED. Hold! Jim; none of that. The die is cast, and I shall abide by my fate. (*Looking off.*) Gipsy is returning, so conceal yourself. I would see her alone.

MONROE. All right, Ned. I shall not trouble you unless I think I can cut you out. (*They exit* R. I E.)

(GIPSY *enters* L. 3 E.)

GIPSY. I've come. Why, where are you ? (NED *enters* R. I E.) Oh, there you are. (*Runs to meet him.*) Now haven't I been a real good Gip to return so soon ?

NED (*kissing her*). You are always good to me, Gip, better than I deserve. Will it continue, think you, through the lapse of years that shall roll between us ?

GIPSY. Oh, Ned, you are not going away ?

NED. Yes, Gip ; to-night, after securing what clothing I shall need, I strike out into the world. (GIPSY *about to speak*. NED *places his hand over her mouth*.) Hold, now ; don't upbraid me. Remember, it is for the best.

GIPSY. But it is wicked of you to leave me alone. If you go away, I shall never see you again, never.

NED. Yes, you will, Gip, if you will do as I wish. Cheer up and let me ask you a question. Will you answer it as I desire ?

GIPSY. Perhaps. I hadn't ought to, though. It would serve you just right.

NED. Never mind that. From the hour Squire Crosby found you a little waif by the way-side, and took you in, I have always liked you. We have grown up as children together — only my father's farm between his cottage and yours. I like your wild and roving ways ; the witticisms of your speech ; your love of the woods, and flowers, and birds —

GIPSY. And animals, too, Ned. Why, I frightened Matilda nearly to death the other day by carrying in a mouse by the tail. Just think of it ! right by the tail.

NED. Oh, hang the mouse ! Tell me if you will be true to me while I am away ?

GIPSY. Certainly ; but you won't go now, will you ?

NED (*impatiently*). Gipsy, you refuse to believe me. As sure as the sun rises and sets I quit this place to-night. I have sworn to never return, and I never will until years have rolled between us, and I am independent with a fortune of my own.

GIPSY. But this quarrel originated through your own fault.

NED. I admit all that. Nevertheless, I shall not return.

If I am a rough stick, it is better I should keep out of the way.

GIPSY. You have never been rough to me, Ned ?

NED. No; God bless you, Gip! I have never harmed you by word or deed. (*Kissing her.*) There! now give me my promise, and I am off.

GIPSY. Why, you have it already.

NED. Have I ? Perhaps I have; but you gave it so lightly, you know. Good-bye, Gip, I will see you again to-night. Until then, farewell. (*Kisses her, and rushes off* R. I E.)

GIPSY (*goes* R. I E. *and looks off*). O dear! when he is gone the world will seem like a great, big, empty kettle. I don't believe he'll go, though. If I did, I'd sit right down here ker-plump (*sits down*) and cry. (*Laughing.*) I don't care! I feel sober if I do laugh.

(*Enter from* L. 3 E., UNCLE NATHAN *and* SQUIRE CROSBY *talking.*)

UNCLE NATHAN. Squire, let us shake. (*They shake hands.*) The jinin' of your darter ter my son has sealed a bond 'o friendship atween us that ought ter last a lifetime. As Davy Crocket would say, "May I be shot!" if I don't hope it will.

CROSBY. Yes — yes, I hope so; but connected with a wedding, it is mighty expensive. A hundred dollars wasted on gewgaws and knickknacks that are of no account. Just think of it.

GIPSY (*aside*). Just think of it. W-h-e-w !

UNCLE N. Well, Squire, the gal is off your hands now, gewgaws an' all. Ain't ye glad ? I — I reckon ye are, Squire. You're rid of a bill of expense. I tell ye, Crosby, yer don't look at wealth in the right light. Why, if I had money — money like as you have, I — I — I'd scatter it all around a-tryin' ter make other people happy. Hang me! if I wouldn't.

CROSBY. And live a pauper all your days. Ah, no; Give me gold — gold. I love to see it glitter; feel its magic touch in my hand; stack it up in piles; shake it, and hear it jingle. There's music in the sound — music. Save money, Nathan; save money. Hoard it up — keep it. When you are old, you can count it, gloat over it —

GIPSY (*imitating him*). Butter it and eat it. Give me money, or — Oh, Father Crosby; if I had money, do you know what I would do with it ?

CROSBY (*snappishly*). Yes; throw it to the dogs and die poor.

GIPSY. No I wouldn't, either.

CROSBY. Well, what would you do with it ?

GIPSY. I'd buy a pig.

CROSBY. A pig ? What would you do with a pig ?

GIPSY. Oh, I'd twist its tail and hear it squeal. (*Imitating.*) There's music in the sound — music. (*Laughs.*)

CROSBY. The minx. (*Retires up stage angrily, seats himself on bench R. of C.*)

UNCLE N. (*laughing, and crossing to* GIPSY). Lord bless ye, Gipsy, if yer couldn't crack a joke, you'd die quicker'n Stebben's dog did when he got choked with a bone. Darn me! if you ain't sharp as a razor. (*Chucking her under the chin.*) W-w-why, gal, if I warn't an old man, an' married at that, I'd smack you with a good old fatherly kiss — stick me with Burgundy pitch if I wouldn't.

GIPSY (*looking sober*) Oh, no, Uncle Nathan, you couldn't kiss me to-day, nohow.

UNCLE N. What! couldn't kiss you to-day ? Lord bless ye, gal, what has the day ter do with it ?

GIPSY. Oh, I'm not happy to-day. I'm out of sorts — that's all.

UNCLE N. Out o' sorts ? Why, gal, ye look happy enough. Lord bless ye, I guess ye do. Out o' sorts ? Ha! ha! ha! I — I didn't know you was ever tooken with that disease. What brought it on; biliousness ?

GIPSY. Oh, you know.

UNCLE N. Hey? It ain't that scapegoat son o' mine ? The ungrateful rascal! Not content with abusin' his old father, he must show his wilfulness by slightin' the weddin'. Let him go, Gipsy, let him go. He's not worthy of you. Not worthy of you no more nor a kicking colt is worthy of a new harness. Let him go, I say.

GIPSY (*looking up archly into his face*). Uncle Nathan, won't you forgive him ?

UNCLE N. (*excited*). Forgive him ? *Me* forgive my *son?* B-b-blast it! gal, he should ask *my* forgiveness.

Didn't he abuse me — *me*, his father ? Didn't he, I say ?
Then why should I forgive him ?

GIPSY. Because I love him. If you don't forgive him,
he will never return.

UNCLE N. Let him go, then — let him go. I've loved
my children — I've indulged 'em — I've petted an' babyed
'em ; an' this is my reward for it. Let him go, I say.

GIPSY. But he will never return.

UNCLE N. Won't he ? won't he return ? Er — er — let
him go, then. If he likes roughin' it, an' dissolute companions better than his mother who worships him, or his father,
who 'ud fight for him till he broke the last bone in his
rickerty old body, let him have them. He'll see the difference sometime — sometime, Gipsy.

GIPSY. But, Uncle Nathan —

UNCLE N. I won't — I won't — I won't hear another
word — another word — not a word. He's a jackanapes ! an
impudent rascal ! a dissolute rogue ! a — a —

GIPSY (*jumping up and placing her hand over his mouth*).
Uncle Nathan, Ned is your son. Now don't be angry with
Gip, please don't. Sit right down here and laugh. (*He
tries to release her hand.*) No ; I'm going to hold my hand
right over your mouth until you smile. (*He sits down.*)
There ! (*Looking into his face.*) Are you smiling, Uncle
Nathan ? (UNCLE NATHAN *seen to smile.*) Ha ! ha ! you
are. I knew you couldn't keep angry with me, could you ?

UNCLE N. (*laughing*). Why, gal, what are ye made on
— what are ye made on. Darn me ! if you won't make a
man rave like a tornado, then smooth him all down like the
surface of a lake without a ripple on it. What are ye made
on, Gip ?

GIPSY. Clay, Uncle Nathan. (*Looking off* L.) Ah,
here they come. Let's meet them. (*Catches hold of* UNCLE
NATHAN, *and whirls him over to* L.)

UNCLE N. Hold on — hold on, gal ! you're yankin' the
life clean out of me.

(*Enter from* L. 3 E., QUINCY *and* NELLIE, *followed by* MRS.
BARDWELL, MATILDA, JOE *and others. They scatter to
different parts of the stage.* JOE *comes down* L. QUINCY
and his bride seat themselves L. C.)

GIPSY (L. C.). Oh, Mrs. Bardwell, do scold Uncle Nathan. We've had a quarrel, and made up, and all inside of five minutes.

MRS. B. Just as I expected. I have to keep my eye upon him continually, or he is sure to get into trouble.

UNCLE N. Maria! Maria! don't show me off right afore my new darter-in-law. Doggone it! if it wasn't for you I might be taken for a President. (*Crossing to* NELLIE.) Look a-here, Nellie, you look as slick as a duck in full plumage. Why, I wouldn't mind a-weddin' of ye myself.

MRS. B. Nathan!

UNCLE N. B-b-blest if I didn't forget that you was present. (*All laugh.*) Come, Maria, let's you and I crochet ter a seat, and show less. (*Takes her arm and crosses to seat* R. I E.)

GIPSY (*to* NELLIE). Say, Nellie, do you know what is the matter with Father Crosby?

NELLIE. No; do you, Gipsy?

GIPSY. Yes, he's had a shock.

NELLIE. A shock?

GIPSY. Yes, I shocked him. He'll live through it though. (*Running to* CROSBY *and throwing her arms around his neck.*) Won't you, Father Crosby?

CROSBY. Go away, child. You bother me.

GIPSY (*laughing*). Then I'm like a fly, ain't I? But you are not angry with me, are you?

CROSBY. No; only so much nonsense irritates me. Irritates me, child.

GIPSY (*laughing*). Well, the best remedy for an irritation, that I know of, is sweet oil. (*Laughing, and crossing to* JOE.) Come, Joe, let's wake up the crowd. This is altogether too quiet for a wedding.

JOE. Shure and I'm ov the same moind meself. (*They pass from one to the other, laughing and talking.*)

QUINCY. Yes, let us all be merry. We know not what the morrow may bring forth.

UNCLE N. I reckon ter me it will bring forth a-shearin' o' sheep —

MRS. B. Keep still, Nathan.

UNCLE N. Lord bless ye, Maria, can't a man waddle his tongue without being cruppered?

(MIKE *heard singing off* R. C.)

GIPSY. Hurrah! here comes Mike. Now we'll have some music.

MATILDA. I'd rather hear it thunder than hear an Irishman sing. (*Crosses to* R. C.)

MIKE (*singing*).

> Young Rory O'More courted Kathleen Bawn,
> He was bold as a hawk, she soft as the dawn,
> He wished in his heart pretty Kathleen to please,
> And he thought the best way to do that was to tease.
> Now Rory be aisy, etc., etc.

(*Enters* C.)

MIKE. Och! its glad I am to see your swate faces, though it's meself that is tardy in getting here. Upon me sowl I hurried loike a man afther the doctor; but a slight accident debarred me from reaching the wedding in time to kiss the bride.

NELLIE. Did you meet with an accident, Mike?

MIKE. Why, av coorse. Have you noticed this suit? Bad luck to the tailor who stole the goose, if he didn't shave from the cloth, and add to the bill. Consequently, when I put it on it was as tight as a number five shoe on a number eight foot. As I stooped to pick up a bill which I had drapped, there was a gineral breakin' away av the back stiches, which left me in a demoralized condition, I kit tell yeez. "What is that?" sez I. "Only a slight tare," sez he. "Tare an' ages!" sez I, "what's to be done?" "Sthand where you are," sez he, "and I will make an insertion." Begorra, I stood for two mortal hours loike a stationary cigar sign, while he stitched me into proper shape to recave company. Thin what did the dirthy spalpeen do afther the job was complayted, but add onother tin dollars to the bill.

NELLIE. Why, what was that for?

MIKE. For the insertion, av coorse. Did ye iver see the loiks? (*He turns around, and shows large strip of black cloth stitched into back of coat and seat of his pantatoons; all laugh.*)

GIPSY (*laughing*). Why, Mike, you are like Joseph with a coat of many colors.

JOE. Yis, loike a postage stamp — stamped.

MIKE. Av coorse I am. Didn't the spalpeen say,
" Variety was the spice of life ? " Begorra! I had to pay
for the spice. (*Retires up stage. All laugh ; to* NELLIE.)
Arrah, acushla, you look as bloomin' as a shamrock in
spring. Shure it's meself wishes someone had sent a kiss to
yeez through my conveyance.

NELLIE. Oh, never mind that, Mike. I don't need any.

GIPSY. And if she did, Quincy would convey them,
never you fear. Wouldn't you Quince?

QUINCY. Well, I should do my duty; but what about
that song ?

ALL (*together*). Yes, a song! a song!

MIKE. Och! niver yez moind a song till the band is
ready to play. Skippin' the rope is the delight ov ladies,
and the gintlemen ain't slow to indulge in the same enjoy-
ment. (*Taking rope from his pocket.*) Shure it's meself
nades a partner to do honor to the occasion.

GIPSY (*coming forward*). Well, I'm here.

MIKE. Begorra, so you are. I should have known it
without your spakin'. Shure you look as fresh as a pink in
the spring with the dew on it. Now to limber the joints,
an' thin we'll have the song afterwards.

(*Music.* MIKE *and* GIPSY *jump rope, which is swung by*
JOE *and one other. If preferred they can jump separate
ropes swung by themselves. All cheer at close.*)

UNCLE N. (*rising and coming forward*). Look a-here,
now, I wouldn't mind tryin' a hand at that air rope myself.

MIKE (*handing him rope*). Begorra! you kin have the
floor at your own convanyance. Come! form a ring and let
the ould gintleman limber his trotters.

(*They form a half circle with* UNCLE NATHAN *in the center.
All are laughing and talking.*)

MRS. B. (L. 1 E.). Now, Nathan, don't make a fool of
yourself.

UNCLE N. Lord bless ye, Maria, don't be so pesky can-
tankerous. Let me alone, can't ye ? Why, I feel as frisky
as a two-year-old steer. Frisky ? I—I guess I do. I kin
take the kinks out 'o this ere rope quicker'n it took Tom
Hooker ter pop the question. I — 1 — I guess I kin.

GIPSY. Wait! Father Crosby must join us. (*Running down stage to* R. C.) Come! you are wanted in the ring.

CROSBY. Away! Such frivolities are boorish. Racket and confusion without profit.

GIPSY. Oh, well, this is a free show, so come along. (*Leads him into the circle.*)

UNCLE N. Come! I'm getting anxious ter show off. Lord bless ye, I feel all of a nettle, as the boy said jumpin' into 'em arter he'd been in swimmin'. Are ye ready?

MIKE. Av coorse — av coorse. It's on the anxious seat we are, awaitin' the motion ov your rivirence.

(*Music. Business of* UNCLE NATHAN *jumping rope. When he has finished, all cheer and clap their hands.* NATHAN *goes* R. I E.)*.

GIPSY. Now, Mike, let us hear from you.

MIKE. Hear from me, is it? Begorra! I'd be ashamed

---

* NOTE. — If Uncle Nathan wishes to introduce a song at this point, the following dialogue may be used :

GIPSY (*after all have finished*). O listen! I want to say something.

MIKE. Begorra! you always did.

QUINCY. What is it, Gip?

GIPSY. I want Uncle Nathan to sing the first song.

ALL (*cheering*). Hurrah! hurrah! give us a song! a song!

UNCLE N. A song? Me sing a song? Lord bless ye! I sung one once, an' — an' what d'yer s'pose was the result?

JOE. An engagement at fifty dollars a week.

UNCLE N. Hey? Did you say anything?

GIPSY. What was the result, Uncle Nathan?

UNCLE N. Fined five dollars and costs for breakin' the peace.

ALL (*together ; laughing*). Give us the song! Give us the song!

GIPSY (*going to him*). Uncle Nathan, sing us the song, and then we'll introduce Mike. You will, won't you?

UNCLE N. I — I'd du anything ter please ye, Gip ; but a song, I — I —. Howsomever, s'longs this's a weddin', I'll make a fool 'o myself, I'll be cowcumbered if I won't. (*Goes down front.*)

MRS. B. Nathan!

UNCLE N. Maria, will you keep quiet? Lord bless ye! quench a fire when it fust starts, an' you'll save the buildin'. They won't want ter hear me only once — only once, Maria, so here goes :

(*Song introduced.*)

(*At close* UNCLE NATHAN *goes* R. I E. *All shout, "Hurrah for Uncle Nathan" when he has finished singing.*)

UNCLE N. Wa'all Maria, I've lived through it. Passed through the fiery furnace like Shadrach an' Abednego, an' come ont whole. Haven't I, now? Jest look at me an' see. Lord bless ye, when you're asked ter du a thing, don't fidget an' wriggle around like a man hitched ter a hornet's nest, but jest go right ter work an' do it. Jest du it, I say.

MRS. B. Then, Nathan, will you please sit down here and keep quiet?

UNCLE N. Hey? Why, sartin'—sartin' I will, Maria. Why didn't ye speak about it afore? (*Sits down.*)

ov meself to refuse afther the present occasion. Jest make shure that you all kin sthand it, an' I'll open wid all me batteries.

(MIKE *introduces song if desired. When he has finished they all cheer and shout for another.*)

MIKE. Och! don't be afther askin' me again, or it's blushing I shall be entoirly. The man who shows himsel! to advantage the first time, better hold that advantage b keeping still.

MATILDA. I motion we go home.

MIKE. Arrah, I'm wid you, Matilda. I'll go wid you.

MATILDA. You won't if I know it.

MIKE. O well! it's not the first toime you've mittened me, so I kin sthand it.

GIPSY. Wait! we must distribute the presents. Go get them, Joe. (JOE *exit* C.)

NELLIE. Am I to be the recipient of presents? Oh, this is a pleasure indeed.

QUINCY. Indeed it is; and for which we express our heartfelt thanks.

MIKE. Don't be afther thankin' for a present until yeez have got it. Begorra! it may fall short of the appreciation of your highness, if I so may be allowed the expression.

GIPSY. Here they come. (JOE *enters* C., *with basket, and advances front.*) Now unpack them, Joe, and let me show them off. (*Business of unpacking presents.* GIPSY *takes them.*) Well, to begin with, here's a cake-knife. (*Reading label.*) From Squire Crosby's hired girl, Matilda. (*Holding it up.*) Isn't it lovely?

NELLIE (*taking it*). Just a little beauty. Oh, thank you, Matilda.

GIPSY (*taking package from* JOE). Then here's a twenty dollar bill. (*Reading label.*) From Uncle Nathan and Maria. (QUINCY *takes it.*)

CROSBY. Ha! extravagance! extravagance!

MIKE. Begorra! I wouldn't moind some ov them presents meself.

GIPSY (*taking package*). And here is a bottle of sooth-ing syrup. (*Reading label.*) From Joe. (*Holds up bottle. All laugh.*)

JOE. Be jabers! the druggist said they moight nade it.

QUINCY (*taking bottle*). And we may, Joe. We will keep it for future reference.

GIPSY. Here is a set of silver knives and forks. (*Reads label.*) From Squire Crosby.

CROSBY. Cost eight dollars — eight dollars in cash.

NELLIE (*taking them and looking them over*). And they are so nice.

MIKE (*aside*). He could pay a hundred dollars to the rest of us a cent and thin have money in the bank.

GIPSY (*taking present*). Oh, what's this ? (*Holding up large doll.*) A doll, as I live ; and presented by Mike. (*All laugh.*)

MIKE. It'll come handy to go with the syrup. Kape it, acushla.

NELLIE (*taking doll*). Indeed, I will ; and with many thanks.

GIPSY. Oh, here's the loveliest present of all. (*Holding up wreath of flowers.*) A wreath of flowers and a necklace. The label reads : " Presented by admiring friends." (*Holding it up.*) Isn't it splendid ?

NELLIE. Oh, how can we ever repay you all ! These presents are more than we deserve.

CROSBY. Altogether. Same amount invested in government bonds would be drawing interest. Good interest.

UNCLE N. Er — er — hang the interest, Crosby, when the principal is makin' others happy. Why, I'd ruther see sunshine on the faces of these young people, an' placed there through my money, than all the cowpons you could stick in a bushel basket. Hang me for a pirate, if I wouldn't.

CROSBY. Folly ! folly ! you are ruined through your generosity, Nathan — your generosity.

UNCLE N. Wa'all I'm purty considerable kind 'o happy, Crosby, an' I kiender cakerlate you ain't.

GIPSY. Let's put these things back in the basket, and then close with a promenade. (*They fill basket.*) Quince, you and Nellie lead off. (*Aside.*) I wish Ned was here.

QUINCY. Certainly. (*Goes down stage,* C.) Now let the rest form on.

MIKE (*to* GIPSY). Come, acushla, would yeez moind racavin' a partner afther the loiks ov meself ?

GIPSY. Why, certainly not. (*All form on except* JOE *and* MATILDA.)

JOE. (*holding basket* R. I E.). Well, where am I ?

MIKE. Begorra, yeez kin have Matilda. I didn't dare ask her meself.

MATILDA (L. I E.). I rather have him anytime than you. (*They form on.*)

(*Music. All promenade.* JOE *in rear with* MATILDA. *He carries basket. When proper,* QUINCY *and* NELLIE *pass out* C., *followed by the others. Scene closes with same song as at opening.*)

NOTE. — *If necessary, the rope jumping can be omitted. In the sentence where* MIKE *says:* "*Och! niver yeez moind a song till the band is ready to play;*" *let* GIPSY *answer:* "*O listen! I want to say something.*" *Then continue. In the same way* MIKE'S *song may be cut, if desired.*

TABLEAU CURTAIN.

SCENE II. — UNCLE NATHAN'S *dooryard. The midnight serenade. Set farmhouse* C. R. *Fence across stage back with gate in center, and country landscape in the distance. If convenient, outhouses to the* L. *If not, set trees. Old-fashioned well near* L. C., *boxed up, and with sweep extending out* L. *Set trees near house with bench in front. Everything to make a farmer's dooryard complete. Square block near* L. C., *front, for seat. As curtain rises,* JOE, MIKE, GIPSY, MATILDA *and others are discovered, with fiddle, horns, drum, pans, etc., giving serenade. Moonlight. For simplicity's sake the set of scene* I *may be used for this scene with dark stage.*

MIKE (C., *to* JOE, *who stands in front of house with fiddle*). Grase thim sthrings, ye spalpeen, or yeez will be afther razin' the whole country. Begorra! they squake loud enough to wake the dead already.

JOE. Shure I'm ov the same moind as yourself, Moike.

(*Chamber window seen to open, and* UNCLE NATHAN, *with night-cap on, looks down upon the crowd. As they continue playing, he quietly withdraws, and soon reappears with blunderbuss, which he pokes out of window, and fires off over their heads. All disappear but* JOE, *who fiddles on undisturbed.*)

UNCLE N. (*looking down at* JOE). Helloa, you, there! ain't yer hit ?

JOE (*playing*). Be jabers! I am ; but the fiddle ain't.

UNCLE N. I should know it — I should know it. Say, now, jest stop that consarned racket, an' — I'll treat the hull crowd.

MIKE (*rushing out from behind fence, followed by the others*). Begorra! I'm wid you, as the tail said to the cat. UNCLE NATHAN *disappears.*)

UNCLE N. (*appearing in doorway buttoning suspenders, and with candle in his hand. Night-cap still on*). W-w- what's goin' on here ? Ain't a fire anywheres, is there ?

GIPSY (*coming down*). Hallo! Uncle Nathan.

UNCLE N. (*shading his eyes with his hand*). Hey ? You here ? Well, well this beats all natur. Everybody broke loose jest like the dogs of Rome.

GIPSY. Did you intend to shoot us, Uncle Nathan ?

UNCLE N. Did I ? Well, now, that's a purty for'ard question. A-a-ain't shot riz in market ? Couldn't waste a charge for nuthin', could I ? Lord bless ye, Gip, if you'd been in front of that air gun, it ud a-blowed ye into kingdom come as sure as natur.

MATILDA. O my!

MIKE. Hould on, Matilda, the ould gintleman was jokin'.

UNCLE N. Wa'all I s'pose you are arter that air son 'o mine an' his new bride ?

MIKE. Begorra, yeez have hit the nail on the head the first toime.

UNCLE N. (*shouting inside*). Maria! Maria! ain't them young people out o' bed yet ?

MRS. B. (*inside*). Yes, Nathan, they will be there shortly.

UNCLE N. Jest tell 'em it ain't perlite ter keep company waitin'. (*Comes down.*) Wa'all, the night is the same, an' the crickets chirrup jest as nat'ral as they did when I was a yengster, an' — an' went on a racket like this myself. Jest sech a racket precisely.

GIPSY. You didn't wear that cap, did you, Uncle Nathan?

UNCLE N. (*placing his hand on his head*). Hey ? Have I got my cap on ? Sure enough! Wa'all, I'm forgetful, ye see ; but I'll take it off ter please ye. (*Takes off cap.*)

(QUINCY *and* NELLIE *appear in doorway. All cheer.*)

QUINCY. Good evening, friends. Allow me to present my bride. (*Leads* NELLIE *down steps.*)

MIKE. And it's quite presentable she is with the moonlight fallin' on her features. Shure I wouldn't moind shakin' hands for the friendship I bear yeez.

(*All shake hands laughing and talking.*)

QUINCY (*after the greeting is over*). Now follow me into the house and we will give you the best the larder affords. (*All cheer, and rush toward house.*)

MIKE. Come, Matilda, I'll show you in.

MATILDA. All right, Michael.

UNCLE N. (*stopping* JOE, *and taking fiddle from him*). Here! don't for the life of ye take that air thing into the house.

JOE (*exhibiting surprise*). What the divil is the matter?

UNCLE N. (*placing it on bench*). Why, the pesky thing might get wound up agin, an' if it did it ud never stop. (*Laughing.*) Go on, Joe, it's all right — it's all right. (*All exit into the house.*)

(*Music.* NED *enters cautiously from* L.)

NED. Now is the time to act. While they make merry within, I can steal into the window, secure my apparel, and escape unobserved. (*Laughter within.*) Hear them laugh! Ten to one if they remember I ever existed. Well, it is only to see ourselves as we really are to know of how little importance we are in the eyes of other people. I wonder if Gip is among them. (*Creeps to window. Singing and laughter continued.*) Yes, there she is, the merriest of the group. Beyond her, seated with her head resting on her hands — Ah, I could tell that form among a thousand. Too often have I pillowed my head upon her breast, listened to her soft caresses, felt her tender kisses upon my lips, to forget the form of that mother who gave me birth. Well, well, I must to business, or I shall find myself at her feet and asking her forgiveness. (*Steals to window* R. H. *front. Singing continued within.*) Let them sing. It will drown the sound of my movements, and prevent my being discovered.

(*Music.* GIPSY *emerges through doorway. Singing continued.*)

GIPSY (*coming front*). Well, I've got out without being missed. Now if I could see Ned, I should feel happy. Seems to me he ought to be here; and if he is here, I ought to see him; and if I do see him, I'll do my best to persuade him to give up his rash purpose. I presume he won't do it, though. O dear! (*Goes down* R. H. *Perceives window open.*) Why, he has been here, and gone. (*Looks into window.*) No; he is on the inside. I'll hide at the corner, and when he passes, I'll make him jump. (*Hides at end of building.*)

NED (*emerging through window with bundle*). Well, I have burglarized my own apartment. Wonder if I should excel in the art if I followed it? (*Closes window.*) Wish I could see Gip for a moment; but time is too precious. The little witch doubts my words, and so may not put in an appearance. (*Passes* GIP *and goes* L.)

GIPSY (*sighing*). O dear!

NED (*starting and looking around*). What! you here? Blest if I noticed you. (*Returns to* GIP.)

GIPSY. I don't think you wanted to.

NED. Yes I did, Gip. Don't imagine I think lightly of you. You are in my thoughts continually. I love you, Gip.

GIPSY. Then why do you leave me?

NED. Under the circumstances I consider it a duty.

GIPSY. Is it a duty to break your mother's heart? Remember, she bore up to-day contrary to her feelings. To-night she has been weeping. (*Crossing to window.*) Look in here, Ned, and you can see her.

NED (*without moving*). I have seen her.

GIPSY. Did the sight not move your heart?

NED (*crossing to her*). Gip, don't talk of such things. I am not here to repent — far from it. What I wish to say relates directly to yourself; and even in that I must be brief.

GIPSY. Then a mother's tears, and the supplications of a sweetheart will not swerve you from your purpose?

NED. No — no; I am firm in my resolve as the pyramids of Egypt. I cannot be moved or shaken. Now let us drop this subject, and speak of yourself. Tell me truly that you love me, and will adhere to me through thick and thin.

GIPSY (*very slowly*). Oh, I couldn't do that, Ned.

NED. What! don't you love me?

GIPSY. O yes; but — but I'm not adhesive, you know.

NED. Gip, stop this joking. If you cannot talk to me as I desire, give me a kiss, and I will be off.

GIPSY. No.

NED (*releasing her hands*). "No?" Do you mean it, Gip?

GIPSY. I do. I am firm in my resolve as — as Gibraltar. I cannot be moved or shaken. Let us —

NED. Very well. (*Moving off.*) I shall not force you against your will. Some one approaches, so farewell. (*Waves his hand and moves off* L.)

GIPSY (*running after him*). Oh, Ned! Ned! I don't mean it, indeed I don't! (*Catches him by lapel of coat and tries to pull him back.*) Come back, please do.

NED (*resisting*). Too late. They are already in the door. Let me go. Quick! (*Trying to release himself.*)

GIPSY (*holding on to coat*). No — no; I won't — I won't —

NED. You must, Gip. (*Wrenches away. Tail to coat tears off.*) There! now farewell. (*Disappears* L. 1 E.)

GIPSY (*almost crying*). Oh, Ned, you are cruel. Gone without a kiss, and all through my own fault. (*Looking at tail to coat.*) Well, I've got so much to remember him by, and I'll keep it, too. (*Puts it into her pocket.*)

UNCLE N. (*emerging through doorway followed by* MRS. BARDWELL). W-w-what is it you've got, Gipsy?

GIPSY (*sneezing*). A cold, Uncle Nathan; and if you remain in this night air, you'll catch one, too.

MRS. B. Gipsy, you have been talking with my boy. Oh, tell me that he has returned?

GIPSY. Yes, he returned; but he has gone again. He left me this to remember him by. Look! Uncle Nathan. (*Shows remnant of coat.*)

UNCLE N. Wa'all, it's as much as I expected, an' — an' a leetle more.

MRS. B. Is it possible, Gipsy, that my boy is deserting his home?

GIPSY. It looks like it. I found him here with bag and baggage. I did my best to dissuade him, but all to no purpose. He was determined to go, and go he did. You noticed this? (*Showing cloth.*) Well, I tore it off while trying to hold him back.

MRS. B. Oh, Nathan, you were too hasty in your reprimand. You must have given away to your temper. Are you sure this was not the case?

UNCLE N. Maria, I am careful of my temper. B-blast it! I haven't got any temper. The boy was impudent — impudent, I say, an' I turned him out of the house.

MRS. B. But you know, Nathan, you get excited too easily. Had you been gentle with him this would not have happened.

UNCLE N. (*growing excited*). B-b-blast it! I was gentle — gentle as a lamb, I tell ye. I told him ter get out of the house; an' an' — an' if he didn't, I would kick him out. That's what I told him, Maria.

MRS. B. But that was not the proper language to use.

UNCLE N. W-w-wasn't it the proper language? Dog rot it! didn't he call me an old fool — me, his father. Didn't he, I say? Is that the language for a child ter use ter a parent? A-a-anything honorable about it? Anything in the commandments that sanctions sech language?

MRS. B. But what did you say? You must have irritated him somehow?

UNCLE N. S'posin' I did — s'posin' I did! Didn't he desarve it? Er — er — hasn't he been devilin' round in bad company? Haven't I cotched him drinkin'? Don't he neglect his duty? Anything about sech conduct ter be proud of? Anything ter make me humble, an' linient, an forget my sense o' duty?

MRS. B. Your duty, Nathan, I do not question. Your mode of performing it I cannot sanction. That boy cannot be driven no more than yourself. You have undertaken it, and now you can see the result.

UNCLE N. Look a-here, Maria, that boy is old enough ter know better. Do you sense it, Maria? Now — now have I got to lead him around with a string as you would a bear, an' teach him his actions? Out upon sech nonsense, Maria! He knows his duty, an' if he can't abide by it, let him go. Let him go, I say.

GIPSY. Uncle Nathan, he is sorry for his conduct, for he

told me so himself. The trouble is, he is too proud to return.

UNCLE N. Too proud, is he? Done wrong, an' — an' ashamed ter own it. Blast it! no man should be too proud ter acknowledge a fault. When he becomes sorry, he'll come back. Don't you fret about that — he'll come back.

GIPSY. Would you welcome him if he should?

UNCLE N. Would I? Why, Lord bless ye, Gip, I'd welcome him with open arms. Don't I love that boy? I — I — reckon I do. That's no reason, though, that I should make a fool of him? No reason that I should let him twist me around his finger — no reason at all.

MRS. B. Don't you think it your duty to see him and persuade him to return?

GIPSY. Oh, do, Uncle Nathan.

UNCLE N. (*excited*). M-Maria, you've said enough. You — you've all said enough. Blast it! do you want me to make a fool of myself? Ask him ter come back? I — I — I'll see him him hanged fust. I'll see him in Halifax. (*Crosses to block* C. L. *and sits down.*) You've said enough — enough, I say.

MRS. B. But, Nathan —

UNCLE N. H-h-hold on, now, I won't hear another word — not a word. I won't be apron-stringed, I tell ye. Enough of a thing is enough whether you like it or not. Let me alone.

GIPSY (*dryly*). I guess if the weather holds we shall have a storm. Don't you, Mrs. Bardwell? (*Laughter within.*) Hello! here comes the crowd. Now, Uncle Nathan, if we don't have you laughing inside of five minutes then Gipsy is no prophet. (MRS. BARDWELL *seats herself.* R. C. GIPSY C.)

(*Enter* MIKE, JOE, QUINCY, NELLIE, MATILDA *and others from house.*)

MIKE. Now that we've rousted the new bride, and feasted, and imptied the ould gintleman's cider jug, I feel loike takin' a quiet departure. (*To* GIPSY.) How is it with yourself, acushla?

GIPSY. Well, if you've got all there is in the house, I might second the motion.

MATILDA. If he didn't it was his own fault.

JOE. Be jabers, he hunted hard enough.

MIKE. Och! didn't I lave you the jug that contained the cider?

JOE. Shure and that was all you did lave, for there was no cider in it.

MIKE. Arrah! did yeez iver see the jug that was capable ov kaping full? Show me the loiks, and I'll own it, handle and all, if I have to stale it.

QUINCY. Look here, my friends, don't think to get off so easily. You have made merry within, now make merry without, and wake up the birds, and let them know that this is a night of rejoicing.

ALL (*together*). A song! a song! a song!

JOE. Yis, sing the Doxology.

GIPSY (*runs to* UNCLE N. *and throws her arms around his neck*). Can I see a smile on your face in the moonlight? You are not angry now, are you?

UNCLE N. I — I'm thawin', I guess. Lord bless ye, how can a man keep angry with so much sunshine around him.

GIPSY. Moonlight, Uncle Nathan.

UNCLE N. H-h-hey? Wa'all, what's the difference when you don't know it?

GIPSY. Will you sing, Uncle Nathan?

UNCLE N. I'll sing at it — I'll sing at it, Gip. Lord bless ye, I'd stand on my head ter please ye. (*All cheer, and call for* UNCLE NATHAN.) Wa'all if I must, I — I s'pose I must. So here goes, as the boy said when he slid off from the roof.

SONG. — "*Voices of the Farm.*"

(*This is less a song than a recitation, having been chanted or intoned by the original performer to a tune and rhythm of his own with great effect.*)

Ho! fair Ceres, ho!
  'Tis early morn and the day is fair;
Up from the valley fog is lifting.
  "Drive those cattle from cornfield, there!"
"Sic 'em, Tige!" on the air comes drifting.
Tin-pails, cowbells, and tools keep a-clattering.
  Whang! in the distance goes a gun.
All such sounds of manual labor
  Show quite plainly, day has begun.
Ho! Joseph Murphy, limber up your fiddle!

Let us make the old welkin ring!
The birds, and beasts, and the little insects
All will delight to dance and sing.
Stand upon a hilltop, on a summer morning,
Not one sound will your quick ears miss,
Lowing of the cattle, cooing of the house-dove,
And in the distance such sounds as this:
Ker-dake! ker-dake! ker-dake! ker-dake! ker-dake! ker-dake!
Such sounds as these will the senses thrill
On a summer morning, calm and still.

Ho! fair Ceres, ho!
The hour is noon, and the sun is high;
Grass in the wind gently waving.
Swallows chitter in a cloudless sky —
Quack! go the ducks in waters laving.
Turkeys, and geese, and hens keep a chattering —
Down in the barn a rooster crows;
Here that juvenile wind-mill turning
Rattle-te-bang! in the wind that blows.
Hark to that sound — oh! that heavenly music!
What can thrill like a dinner horn!
Hurrah! hurrah! the echoes answer,
Out from the fields of grain and corn.
Stand upon a hill top, on a summer noon-day,
Not one sound will your quick ears miss;
Going home from labor, driving yokes of oxen,
And the words you hear will sound like this:
Gee — gee off there, Buck! Haw! Whoa-hish! whoa-hish! — Star-
line!
Such sounds as these will the senses thrill
On a summer noon-day calm and still.

Ho! fair Ceres, ho!
The day is done, and the sun is set;
Dew on the grass is softly falling.
Cow-bells tinkle in the distant lot —
Crows to their mates are harshly calling.
Crickets in the grass keep cherruping, cherruping.
Hark! in the swamp the night-birds sing.
Whip-poor-will, cat-bird, thrush and sparrow —
Whir-r-r! goes a shooting night-hawk's wing.
Ho! father long-legs! seated on a thistle!
Hear his legs on his silk wings grind!
The toads, and the frogs, are wierdly croaking —
All kind of noises seem combined.
Stand upon a hill-top, on a summer evening,
Not one sound will your quick ears miss;
Barking of the house-dog, rustle of a leaflet,
And from the pasture such sounds as this:
Co-boss! co-boss! co-boss! co-boss! co-boss! co-boss!
Such sounds as these will the senses thrill
On a summer evening, calm and still.

(*When he has finished, all shout: "Hurrah for Uncle
Nathan!"* UNCLE NATHAN *crosses* L.)

MIKE. Begorra! the whole farm was worked into that
conglomeration but jest the ould oaken bucket and the cat.
Thim two articles was left out entoirly.

JOE. And one other thing.

MIKE. Indade! would yeez be afther explaining what?

JOE. Mike O'Connor, Crosby's hired man.

MIKE. Arrah! yeez are correct, me boy. And the omission of the same is where the piece lost one of its strongest faytures. But, whist! now I think ov it, there's another omission av far more consequence thin the other.

GIPSY. Now, Mike, it is my time to ask what.

MIKE. An ould toime counthry dance in the dooryard. The ould gintleman couldn't sing it, an' in order to make the thing complayte, and tarminate the night in proper shape, begorra! I motion we act it.

(*Cries of " Yes! yes! — Hurrah! hurrah! -- Virginia Reel! " etc.*)

QUINCY. Nothing could suit me better. Come! let us form on. Nellie and I will take the lead. (*They form on.*)

GIPSY (*crossing to* MIKE *who is down* R. I E.). Come, Mike, have I got to ask you to be my partner?

MIKE. Well, the gintleman who waits for an invitation is niver in danger ov being refused. I'm wid you, acushla.

MATILDA (*stepping in front and taking* MIKE *away*). Well, I guess not.

GIPSY (*laughing*). Good-by, Michael. Come, Joe, I'll take you.

QUINCY (*after all are formed on*). All ready. Commence! (*Music ; dance.*)

(UNCLE NATHAN *becomes excited as the dance progresses, and beats time to the music. At last he dances over to* MRS. BARDWELL *who is seated* R. C. *back.*)

UNCLE N. Maria! I — I can't stand it! Come! let us dance. (*Catches hold of her.*)

MRS. B. Oh, Nathan! I don't feel like dancing.

UNCLE N. But — but you must, Maria. Lord bless ye, I'm young again clean ter the back bone. Come! come along. (*He pulls her into set. All dance, during which curtain falls.*)

(*Eleven years supposed to have elapsed between the first and second acts.*)

ACT II.

SCENE I. — *Nathan Bardwell's dooryard, same as in Act I., Scene I. As curtain rises,* UNCLE NATHAN *and* BELLE *are discovered seated on a bench* R. C., *under tree.* NATHAN *is much older in appearance, and goes with cane. Time — morning.*

UNCLE N. (*relating story*). Now the collier lived in a cottage that was haunted by a terrible specter. This specter hated wicked people, an'— an' when they wus around him, he used ter grow till he looked like a great big giant; but if the people around him wus good, he used ter shrink until he warn't no bigger nor nuthin'.

BELLE. Was he a great big giant when the man lived in the cottage ?

UNCLE N. Yes; for the man who lived there before him was wicked. This made the specter so large that he drove the man away. But the collier was good, ye see, an'— an' so the specter shrunk, an' shrunk, until he warn't no bigger nor you are; an' he shrunk, an' shrunk, until he warn't no bigger nor a pea; an' at last he shrunk away altogether.

BELLE. And did he ever come back ?

UNCLE N. No; he couldn't, ye see, for the collier was good. But he left his presence there, in the shape of a gentle light, an'— an' sweet strains of music, that wus soft an' low, an' pleasant ter hear. This made the old collier so happy, that he used to call this presence his " house spirit."

BELLE. Do you have such a spirit, grandpa ?

UNCLE N. I — I cakerlate that everybody who is good has sech a spirit, Belle.

BELLE. Was you always good, grandpa ?

UNCLE N. Wa'all, I — I try ter be, Belle, I try ter be. I may fall short once in a while; but I try ter be good. Haven't I been good ter you, Belle ?

BELLE. Oh, yes, indeed you have; and you love me, too, don't you ?

UNCLE N. Yes, Belle; I've loved ye for ten years, goin' on. You see, Quincy, your father, is dead, an'— an' your mother is dead, so I haven't any other children but you to love.

BELLE. You have Uncle Ned ?

UNCLE N. Nuthin' certain about him, Belle, nuthin' certain at all. He may be alive, or he may be dead, the Lord only knows. I know I still pray for him, an' if there's any vartue in prayer, he'll come back sometime, Belle — he'll come back sometime.

BELLE. Grandma don't think he will; but Gipsy does.

UNCLE N. Yes; Gipsy still looks for him. Lord bless ye, I guess she does. But he don't desarve her — don't desarve her in the least. There! run in now, while I talk with Mike. I see him coming up the walk, an' it may be Crosby that sent him.

BELLE (*jumping up and throwing her arms around his neck*). I don't like Grandpa Crosby one bit. He is cross and says hateful things to me, and once he boxed my ears and called me a brat. You don't do that, do you ? Now let me kiss you. (*Kisses him, then runs to door.*) Good-by, grandpa. (*Throws kiss at him, then runs into house.*)

UNCLE N. (*laughing*). Lord bless her! Wa'all, if a purson ain't appreciated in this world, it's purty apt ter be his own fault — his own fault. (*Enter* MIKE, C.) Good mornin', Mike.

MIKE. Mornin' to yourself, your honor, and to the house. May I ask if your riverence is in comfortable health ?

UNCLE N. Nuthin' ter brag on, Mike, nuthin' ter brag on. Er — er — is Crosby purty well ?

MIKE. Is he well ? Begorra! he's ugly as the divil, and twice as disagreeable. Loike a thistle, the older he grows the more he shows his bad points; an' he has enough ov 'em, I kin tell yeez.

UNCLE N. Soured — soured, I guess; an' the loss of his darter don't sweeten him any. H-hard on Gip, though, mighty hard.

MIKE. Och! niver yeez fear for Gip. It's a fire she has in her eye, an' a tornado in her bosom, an' when she becomes angry, by the Holy St. Patrick! the ould gintleman has to dance to her fiddling, or may I turn into a ghost. Don't yeez have no fears for Gip.

UNCLE N. It may be — it may be. She can hold her own, I guess; an' — an' you seem to.

MIKE. Oh, yiss, your honor; I'm tough. I'm loike an

ould iron target. I've been battered so much that I have no scars, and don't moind being shot at. Shtill, and it's mesilf that's ashamed to own it, I am battered in a direction that makes me wilt complaytely.

UNCLE N. H-hey? Battered in another direction?

MIKE. Yiss, your rivirence, and badly, too. Be aisy now, and I'll be afther giving yeez a bit ov advice. If yeez iver become single, don't marry a girl in her 'teens, or out ov your own nationality. Begorra! if ye do, yeez will wish ye had niver made the mistake ov being born. I do already.

UNCLE N. W-w-what's that! Your marriage with Matilda a failure? I didn't mistrust it.

MIKE. Arrah! it's because yeez are not posted. I thry to kape up appearances; but it's moity hard work, I kin tell yeez. The shmile on a man's face is often a mantle to the frown that rankles in his bosom; an' — I apply that to me own case. Now this gold excitement —. Och! and have yeez heard about thim foinding gold in Rocky Run?

UNCLE N. (excited). W-w-what's that! Gold in Rocky Run? Gold in my pasture?

MIKE. The identical same, your honor. The whole ov New England has got the gold faver worse thin Californy, and ivery mither's son is out wid a tin pan a-washin' for it. Well, last week, two men what they call pros—pec—tus, sthruck the color over in Crosby's lot, and yisterday they made a big foind in the sthream that crosses your own land.

UNCLE N. Y-y-you don't mean it! you don't mean it! By John Rogers! you don't mean it!

MIKE. Arrah! it's a fact, your honor. I saw it wid my own two blissed eyes, in the bottle where they kept it secrayted.

UNCLE N. A-a-and it wus gold — real gold?

MIKE. It was that, and as bright as a dandelion blossom. They will be afther calling upon ye to-day; an' it's meself would loike Joe to help sarch the shtream more complaytely, if yeez don't moind sparing him for the toime being.

UNCLE N. You kin have him — you kin have him. D-d-drat it! kin they have found gold on my land? I — I — I can't believe it.

MIKE. Well, I heard thim say it, your honor, and thin there was the samples in the bottle. But I've got off from me subject entoirly. This gold excitement, as I started to say, raised the divil with Matilda complaytely. Nothing would do but I must dig the whole counthry over, and all for a mine, that — begorra! kin only exist in her own divilish imagination.

UNCLE N. A-a-and have you ever found any gold, Michael?

MIKE. Niver a speck, your honor. Shure it's meself wishes I had in order to kape pace in the family. For now it's "Moike" here, and "Moike" there and "Moike, I must have money," and "Moike, if yeez was as smart as other men," and — Begorra! here she comes now. Look at her! (*Points off* C.) Every dollar I kin rake an' shcrape put upon her back to make her look foine. (*Goes* L. 1 E.) Och! but I shall cotch it now.

MATILDA (*enters* C., *whistling*. *Perceives* MIKE). You here, are you? Didn't I tell you I must have ten dollars? Is this the way you are trying to earn it?

MIKE. Shure I intend —

MATILDA. Intend! intend! you always intend. (*To* NATHAN.) Oh, Mr. Bardwell! he's the laziest good for nothing you ever saw.

UNCLE N. Wa'all — er — er — I've known him —

MATILDA. Yes, you've known him; but you don't know his peculiarities as I do. Why, he makes a perfect drudge of me. I actually have had to wash my own dishes for the past six weeks.

MIKE. Begorra! yeez have kept me digging for gold —

MATILDA. Shut up! I will do the talking myself. If you've been digging for gold, where is it? Show me a sample? Other men find gold, and give it to their wives. Where is yours?

MIKE. Shure I —

MATILDA. Oh, don't go to making excuses. I know the reason — you don't try. Other men hunt for it while you lie around in the sun and doze. That's all your good for. Mr. Bardwell, what would you do with such a lazy lout of a husband if you were in my place?

UNCLE N. B-b-by John Rogers! I'd respect him. I — I —

MATILDA. Respect him? Ha! ha! ha! respect such a

thing as he is. Just look at him, now. (*Goes L. Takes* MIKE *by the ear and leads him front.*) Isn't he a picture in a frame? Look at that attitude? Isn't it graceful? (*Throwing him off.*) Oh, you wretch! I've no patience with you.

UNCLE N. (*getting angry*). B-blast it! man, assert your rights — assert your rights!

MIKE. Shure I —

MATILDA (*stamping her foot*). Don't you speak. Ha! ha! ha! assert his rights! I should just like to have him try it. Just let him try it.

MIKE. Jhust one word if you plaze —

MATILDA. Shut up! I tell you. Start your boots to work. What are you doing here anyway?

MIKE. Afther Joe, mam.

. MATILDA. A pretty excuse. (*Points off* C.) You march! do you hear?

MIKE (*going*). Yiss — yiss, mam. I'm traveling. (*Goes off* C.)

MATILDA. I'll settle with you when we arrive at the house. Oh, Mr. Bardwell, he tries me so, I have no patience with him. Sometimes I wish I might die, and then I should be at peace. (*Exit* C., *scolding.*)

UNCLE N. (*to himself excitedly*). I — I should want you to — I should want you to. B-blast it! if you was my wife, I — I — I — I — Well, I wouldn't have sech a wife — I wouldn't have sech a wife. (*Calling.*) Maria! Maria!

MRS. B. (*opening door*). Well, Nathan.

UNCLE N. They've struck gold in Rocky Run. What d'yer think of it! What d'yer think of it, Maria?

MRS. B. Don't be deceived, Nathan. My advice is to be careful.

UNCLE N. Oh, I — I'll be careful. Can't see no harm, in findin' gold, blest if I can. W-w-why, if reports are true, they are findin' it all around us — all around us, Maria.

MRS. B. The reports may be exaggerated.

UNCLE N. They may be. It's best ter be careful — I admit that; but if there's gold in the gulch, we are rich, Maria, rich as Jews.

MRS. B. I am contented as it is. Don't get excited, Nathan, until you have some reason.

UNCLE N. No; I'll be calm. B-b-blast it! I'm always calm, Maria. But the gold — er — er — Mike has seen it — seen it in the bottle.

MRS. B. Well, let us wait for the result. (*Looking off* c.) Crosby and two strangers are coming up the lane. You know how that man figures for your farm, so don't get caught in any scheme.

UNCLE N. Oh, I'll be careful, I tell ye. Don't be afeared. I'll handle 'em as I would a pair o' hot tongs — hot tongs, Maria.

MRS. B. If you will, we shall have nothing to fear. (*Exit into house.*)

(*Enter* CROSBY, MAYHEW *and* BLYNN, C.)

CROSBY (*rubbing his hands*). Good morning, Nathan. Allow me to introduce Charles Mayhew and Richard Blynn, assayers and prospectors. Gentlemen, Mr. Nathan Bardwell. (*All bow, etc.*)

BLYNN. Happy to meet you, Mr. Bardwell.

MAYHEW. Which pleasure also affords gratification to myself.

UNCLE N. (*suspiciously*). I — I — I suppose so — I suppose so. Er — er — help yourselves ter some seats, gentlemen. (*All seat themselves but* CROSBY.)

BLYNN. I have the pleasure, Mr. Bardwell, of informing you of the discovery of placer gold in Rocky Run, as well as some rare specimens taken from the adjacent rocks; nearly all of which, as Mr. Crosby informs me, were found within the precincts of your own land.

CROSBY (*rubbing his hands together*). Gold, Nathan, gold. Rich, red and radiant gold. There it lies, sparkling among the pebbles of the brook; your brook and mine, Nathan. There it lies, hidden away, waiting for eager hands to gather in. Think of it, Nathan.

BLYNN. We have samples with us just as they were taken from the brook. From indications, there must be a rich pocket, or deposit, somewhere in the immediate vicinity. We are certain of this, though the locality has not quite been determined.

CROSBY. Show him the gold. Show him the samples in the bottle. (MAYHEW *hands bottle of samples to* NATHAN.) Look at it, Nathan. How it glimmers, glitters, sparkles in the sun! How radiant, beautiful it looks! Ha! don't it make you feel young again? Don't it make your fingers tingle and your heart burn? It is yours — yours, Nathan. The samples were found on your land, and are yours.

MAYHEW. So far as I can learn, we have made the richest find in New England. Of course this is confidential. The samples already found, at a rough estimate, are worth, at least, two hundred dollars.

UNCLE N. Y-y-you don't mean it! you don't mean it!

CROSBY. We do, Nathan; and all of it, every mill, and fractional part of a mill belongs to you.

BLYNN. Recollecting, of course, that we claim a nominal per cent as the discoverers.

UNCLE N. B-b-by John Rogers! if you've found gold on my land, you shall be paid for it — well paid for it, I say.

CROSBY. I told them so. I knew you would do your duty by them. It's worth remunerating — eh! Nathan?

MAYHEW. It is not so much the remuneration we ask for, as it is to come to some understanding. Of course our proposition would be, to purchase the land outright. This, Mr. Crosby informs me, cannot be done.

UNCLE N. No sir — no sir. You couldn't buy my farm if you should kiver every foot of it with bank bills. It's a home farm, sir. A farm on which I was born, an' on which the father afore me was born. I love the old farm, sir; an' — an' I intend ter keep it.

CROSBY. I told them so, Nathan.

BLYNN. Realizing this fact, Mr. Mayhew and myself have come before you with a proposition. We are confident that a rich deposit of gold is hidden in Rocky Run. We have proof of this from the samples in the bottle. Now —

UNCLE N. The proposition — give me the proposition.

BLYNN. Mr. Mayhew, repeat the proposition as arranged between ourselves.

MAYHEW. It is this. You and Mr. Crosby advance five thousand dollars, and Mr. Blynn and myself will put in the proper machinery, and work the claim for twenty per cent of the gross receipts. The agreement is already drawn up, and to which Mr. Crosby has affixed his signature. Understand me, we make this extraordinary offer on account of our inability to purchase the land. Were this possible, and with our confidence in the richness of the find, we would prefer to pay for all rights and privileges and work the claim on our own responsibility.

UNCLE N. But, Lord bless ye, w-w-where's the money? Kin I perform a miricle like the prophets? I haven't a dollar in cash ter my name.

CROSBY. I'll advance the money, Nathan.

UNCLE N. W-w-what's that ter me? What's that ter me?

CROSBY. Ahem! I'll explain. (*Takes papers from his pocket.*) Here are documents — legal documents — documents officially made out and witnessed. Here is the agreement with my name attached. Read it, Nathan. (*Hands him agreement.*) Here is another document — a note — payable in one year. (*Hands him note.*) Affix your name to that, and I'll advance the money, Nathan.

UNCLE N. Where's your security? Y-y-you want security, don't ye?

CROSBY. Oh, the farm will be the security. It is one of the conditions of the note. See? Sign the note, Nathan, and I'll risk the security.

UNCLE N. (*throwing him back the papers*). N-n-no — no. I'll not do it. By John Rogers! I'll not do it. I've been there before. I'll see you hanged fust! I'll not do it, I say.

BLYNN. My dear sir, do you imagine that you are assuming a risk?

UNCLE N. Don't I risk my farm? D-d-don't I risk it, I say?

CROSBY. But the gold, Nathan. Ah! think of the gold.

UNCLE N. D-d-dog gone it! how do I know there is any gold! Have I seen it dug? Have I any proofs of it beyond your own words?

MAYHEW. Mr. Bardwell is right. You, Mr. Crosby, have looked the matter over. He must do the same. First, what is the private value of your farm?

UNCLE N. I don't value it, sir; it's beyond value.

CROSBY. The appraisal is five thousand dollars. I have offered him seven within a year.

MAYHEW. Very good. So confident am I of a fortune in Rocky Run, that, if you will deed me your farm, with all rights and privileges, I will pay you ten thousand dollars for it before the sun shall set.

UNCLE N. (*jumping up, excited*). W-w-what! Ten thousand dollars for my farm! You kin have it! (*Recollecting himself.*) N-n-n-n-*no* — NO — NO. You can't have it for twice ten and ten on top of that. (*Sinks upon bench.*)

(GIPSY *heard singing off* C. CROSBY *and others show surprise.*)

CROSBY (*aside*). Curses light on that hussey! is she coming here to spoil my scheme. (*Walking toward* C.)

GIPSY (*singing outside*). Tra-la! tra-la! — tra-la-la-la! tra-la-la-la-la-la! (*Enters* C. *Perceives* CROSBY *and the others.*) La-a-a-a-an! O my! (*Goes* L. I E., *dragging her hat behind her.* BLYNN *and* MAYHEW *bow and retire* R. I E. CROSBY *follows* GIPSY L. I E.)

CROSBY (*hissing in her ear*). What are you here for — eh?

GIPSY (*carelessly*). To bother you, I guess. Ha! ha! it seems to, don't it? (*Crossing to* NATHAN.) Good morning, Uncle Nathan. You didn't notice me, I guess.

UNCLE N. Yes, yes, I noticed you — I noticed you; but I wus mixed up, Gipsy. I shall be all right in a minute.

(CROSBY *keeps talking and gesticulating to* GIPSY L. I E., *while* BLYNN *and* MAYHEW *are talking.*)

BLYNN (*aside to* MAYHEW R. I E.). Mayhew, something about that girl troubles me. It did yesterday when I talked with her. A look, or something that relates to the past.

MAYHEW. Perhaps you are captivated, like myself. Say! you transact the business and let me attend to the girl.

BLYNN. Very well. Let us make another start, and then I'll excuse you.

(*They cross to* NATHAN *and engage him in conversation.*)

GIPSY (L. I E.). Look here, Father Crosby, you can gesticulate and threaten all you want to; you can't frighten me one bit. I'm here to stay, and stay I'm going to.

CROSBY. Ha! is this your obedience? You, a brat whom I picked out of the gutter? Do I not feed and clothe you?

GIPSY. Yes, and abuse me, too; but I'm used to it. I work for you, and obey you in every thing practical; but when it comes to a dishonest action, I'll fight against it with my last breath.

CROSBY. Who is performing a dishonest action?

GIPSY. You are; at least, I mistrust it.

CROSBY. You mistrust it. Ha! is that all?

GIPSY. Well, if your business is honorable, why do you object to my presence?

CROSBY. You have no business here. Remain, though, and listen like a woman at a keyhole, if you want to. Don't you interfere — remember that. Keep your mouth shut. (*Crosses to* NATHAN.)

GIPSY (*aside*). Ha! ha! ha! I've lived through that. Well, I'm getting so I can stand 'most anything. (MAYHEW *approaches.*) Yes, and now I've got to stand being mashed.

MAYHEW (*approaching and bowing*). Fortune favors me in again meeting you, and renewing our conversation of yesterday.

GIPSY. Yes, but I can't speak.

MAYHEW. You can't speak?

GIPSY. No; Father Crosby told me to keep my mouth shut.

MAYHEW (*laughing*). In some cases it is prudent. In this instance, however I think you will be excusable. Indeed! your lips are too pretty to remain hermetically sealed.

GIPSY (*starting*). O my!

MAYHEW. W-what's the matter?

GIPSY. Oh, nothing. Your confession startled me. It took away my breath. A girl in the country, you know, is not used to flattery; and — and it makes me feel so funny. Do you know, to pay you, I've a good mind to give my lips —

MAYHEW (*grasping her hand*). Oh, do — do.

GIPSY (*as if surprised*). Do what!

MAYHEW (*embarrassed*). Why — that is — er — I mean, you spoke of giving your lips —

GIPSY. Oh, yes. Ha! ha! ha! giving my lips a rest. Don't you think it policy, Mr. Mayhew? There! now think of it, I will rest myself. (*Sits on bench* L. I E., *and taking pains to occupy the whole seat.*) Won't you please be seated, Mr. Mayhew?

MAYHEW (*observing no seat to occupy*). No, thanks; I
— I — that is — I prefer standing, I think. (*Aside.*) Con-
found the girl!

GIPSY.   There! how stupid. A girl in the country is so
green. You must put up with my awkwardness, Mr.
Mayhew; but really, I did not observe but what chairs were
plenty.

MAYHEW.   Don't mention it, please.

GIPSY.   Then I won't. You might occupy the end of
this bench, I suppose. (*Moving along and showing very
small portion of seat.*) Will that do, Mr. Mayhew?

MAYHEW.   I fear I should crowd you. (*Aside.*) Blest
if I don't think the girl is poking fun at me.

GIPSY.   Ha! ha! ha! I declare, you might. I didn't
think of that. I tell you, lean against the pump. (*Jumping
up.*) By the way, will you draw me a glass of water,
please?

MAYHEW.   With pleasure. (*Business at pump.*)

BELLE (*appearing in doorway with* MRS. BARDWELL).
Oh, there is Gipsy. (*Running to* GIPSY.) O Gipsy! I am
awful glad to see you.

MRS. B.   Belle, you mustn't say "awful," it isn't pretty.

BELLE.   Well, I won't say it again; but I was awful glad,
wasn't I, Gipsy?

GIPSY (*kissing her*).   Bless your little heart, I guess
you was. (*Business between* GIPSY, MAYHEW, *and* BELLE
at the pump.)

UNCLE N.   M-Maria, come here. Here are the samples
of gold. Look at 'em, Maria; an'-an' at these papers at the
same time. (*Hands her the bottle of samples and the
papers.*) Now they've made me an offer; an offer of ten
thousand dollars for the farm. What d'yer think of it?
W-what d'yer think of it, Maria?

GIPSY (*offering glass of water to* MAYHEW, *who is listening
to* NATHAN; *loudly*).   Take it!

MAYHEW.   Oh, beg pardon. (*Takes glass.*)

CROSBY (*turning upon her fiercely*).   Hush! you minx,
hush. (GIPSY *turns her back upon him*).

MRS. B.   Would it not be better to take that amount,
Nathan, than to run the risk of signing these papers?

UNCLE N.   I won't sell the farm, Maria. It's our home.

A shelter ter us in our old age. It's the place where I wus born; an' I'm goin' ter stick to it if the gold mine in Rocky Run lies buried until etarnity.

BLYNN. Knowing this, Mrs. Bardwell, we make the offer, the conditions of which are upon that paper.

MRS. B. And which, if he signs, will endanger his farm.

BLYNN. Mrs. Bardwell, a fortune lies buried under Rocky Run. My knowledge of this led me to make my extravagant offer for the place. The same knowledge also leads me to make the other proposition.

MRS. B. If you are so positive of this, why do you not, with our consent, work the claim on your own responsibility? We will take the per cent, and let you assume the risk.

UNCLE N. Th-th-that's it, Maria! That's it exactly!

CROSBY. It isn't policy, Mrs. Bardwell. The gold is on my land as well as Nathan's. We own it together. It is ours. Give them the per cent. — eh! why not?

MRS. B. But what positive proof have we that the treasure is such as you claim?

BLYNN. First, in the samples. Second, in our willingness to purchase the farm. Lastly, we ask him to sign no papers until he has investigated for himself.

UNCLE N. That's fair — that's fair, Maria. Nuthin' could be fairer than that.

CROSBY. I assume the same risk, Mrs. Bardwell, as your husband. Two thousand five hundred, the same as he does.

BLYNN. Shall we set to-morrow at ten o'clock as the hour to meet in Rocky Run?

UNCLE N. Yes — yes, I'll be there. I'll look the matter over. I'll be there at ten o'clock.

GIPSY (*to* MAYHEW *who jokingly threatens to sprinkle her with water from the tumbler; loudly*). Don't you do it.

MAYHEW. Beg pardon, I won't. (*Turns water into well.*)

CROSBY (*turning upon her fiercely*). Hush! you minx, hush!

BLYNN. And if everything is proven to your satisfaction you will sign the agreement?

UNCLE N. (*slowly rising to his feet*). I-I-I'll see the gold fust. I'll — see — the — gold—fust. If I kin see it dug — dug right out o' the sand, right out o' the rocks — w-w-why, I'll see, I'll see then.

GIPSY (*quickly turning from pump*). Uncle Nathan! CROSBY *steps in front of her and motions her back*.) I want to speak to Uncle Nathan, and I'm going to. (*Pushing CROSBY aside.*)

UNCLE N. Wa'all, Gipsy, what is it? What is it?

GIPSY. Do you really love the old farm as you pretend?

UNCLE N. Do I love the old farm? Lord bless ye child, haven't I said a thousand times that it ud break my heart ter lose it? That next ter my own family, an' — an' you, Gipsy, that I loved it better than anything else on airth?

GIPSY. You love it so well, don't you, that the ten thousand offered would be no temptation for you to sell it?

UNCLE N. Gipsy, I may be foolish. I'm old, ye know, an' — an' I'm gettin' childish. But in my weakness, an' — seein' things as I do in my dotage, I wouldn't give up this home farm for the hull of King Solomon's temple; I tell ye I wouldn't do it.

GIPSY (*forcibly*). Then, Uncle Nathan, if money will not purchase your farm; if you love it as devotedly as your words imply, don't you sign those papers.

PICTURE.

SITUATION OF CHARACTERS.

UNCLE NATHAN *down* C. R. GIPSY C. *back, with right hand pointing at papers.* MRS. BARDWELL C. R., *holding papers.* CROSBY *stands near* GIPSY *and looks as if he would throttle her.* BELLE *clinging to* GIPSY. MAYHEW L., *near pump, and* BLYNN R. *Both in attitudes exhibiting surprise.*

UNCLE NATHAN

MRS. BARDWELL   GIPSY.

BELLE.

BLYNN.   CROSBY.

(*Pump.*)

MAYHEW.

R.   TABLEAU CURTAIN.   L.

SCENE II. *Rocky Run. Full extent of stage. Mountain drop masked in with set rocks. A stream of water falls* R. U. E., *masked in with set pieces. Tree* L. 2 E . *for* MIKE *to climb into. Hollow log* R. 2 E. *Set trees* L. *and* R. *Enter* JOE *and* MIKE L. 3 E., *each with shovel and pan.*

MIKE (*cautiously going down* C., *followed by* JOE). Whist! be aisy, now. Tread softly an' make no noise, or yeez will be afther raising the divil with fire issuing from his mouth and smoke from his nostrils.

JOE. What the divil is he coming here for?

MIKE. Och! what ignorance yeez be afther displaying. Shure haven't yeez heard how the avil one sthands sintinel over buried treasures, an' to dig for 'em yeez must hould in-can-ter-ray-shuns? Didn't yeez iver hear ov the loikes?

JOE. Shure that is when the treasures are stolen and thin buried. This ain't no Captain Kidd wid his gold, so come along. (*They cross to brook down stage and proceed to work.*)

MIKE. Begorra! yeez are spaking the truth. It was off from the track I was entoirly. (*Washes for gold.*) Well, it relaves me moind loike going to the confessional, and makes me as plazed as when I'm out ov the sight ov Matilda. Och! but I had to cotch it yisterday, I can tell yeez.

JOE. I wouldn't shtand it.

MIKE. Wouldn't sthand it? Shure can I be afther doing any different? Is there any power kin shtop a woman's tongue when she has a moind to use it? I mane, any power outside from death, an' the usual stroke of paralysis.

JOE. Be jabers! I'd put a gag in her mouth.

MIKE. Yiss; but what would Matilda be doing the mane toime?

JOE. Why did ye marry her in the first place, Moike?

MIKE. Och! she was different thin. Before marriage, it was, "Me own swate Moike;" and, "Mike, I love yeez;" and, "Moike, I should die without yeez;" and thin the swatest av kisses she would give me, until — by the sowl ov me — it is carried away I was complately. But now — och, murther! — (*Starting, and dropping pan,*) Did yeez hear that?

JOE (*dropping and listening*). What was it, Moike?

MIKE. Begorra! I should loike to foind out meself.
Didn't yeez hear a wheezing noise up there among the rocks,
loike a man wid the phthisic, or some ould gintleman
snorin'? (*Looks up among rocks.*)

JOE. I didn't, Moike.

MIKE. Shure then you must be deaf as Baalam's ass. Indade! its meself that belaves that digging for gold is tickel-
ish business.

JOE (*picking up pan*). Yeez are superstitious, Moike.
(*Business washing for gold.*)

MIKE. Well, I may be loike the ould woman who heard
a burglar in the house when she didn't. Sure if the noise
I heard was not a noise, then the noise I heard must have
been a noise I imagined. Anyhow, here goes for a thousand
dollar nugget. (*Business with pan and shovel.*)

JOE. Yeez are not mistaken about this being the place,
Moike?

MIKE. Av coorse I am not. Don't the land up yonder
(*Pointing off* L. U. E.) belong to Crosby, an' don't the land
here belong to Bardwell, an' didn't they foind gold both
sides ov the line? Thim rocks up there (*Pointing off* R. U.
E.) is where they found the quartz. Och! and I've heard
them tell all about it when they thought I was slayping.

JOE (*examining piece of ore*). Say, Moike, is this gold?

MIKE (*looking at ore*). Shure yeez are a bigger fool thin
O'Harry was whin he thried to put out a cigar wid his tongue.
Tare an' ages! can't yeez tell gold from jasper? (*Throwing
ore away.*) Begorra! there's no more gold in that thin
there was in the crap of Tom Piper's goose when he killed
it. Say, did yeez iver hear the story ov Tom Piper's goose?

JOE. I never did, Moike.

MIKE. Well, Tom Piper dhramed three toimes that if he
would take his ould pet goose at midnight down into a cavern in the big woods, an' kill it, an' thin build four fires at
right angles, and sprinkle the four fires wid absinthe, an'
thin kneel between them, an' say, " I, Tom Piper belaving in
ghosts an' witches, and that they can convart sthones into
gold, do hereby sacrifice the body ov my pet goose, an'
acknowledge myself a belaver, etc," he could open the crap
— after the body was consumed, remember — and it would
be filled with bright, yellow nuggets ov gold.

JOE. An' did Tom Piper do it?

MIKE. Yiss; afther dhraming the same thing for three nights, he took the ould goose on the midnight av the fourth, an' went to the cavern. Begorra! it was a pokerish place, I kin tell yeez. There was bats, and snakes, and bugs, and adders, and ivery thing else that made Tom Piper's flesh crape loike the skin ov an eel over a hot fire. But he killed the goose, and built the four fires, and sprinkled them with absinthe, and knelt between them, and said: "I, Tom Piper, belaving in ghosts, and witches—" (*Shriek, or hooting of owl heard among rocks off* C.) Holy St. Patrick! (*Drops pan, rushes around stage, and off behind rock* L. U. E.)

JOE. The divil is afther us. (*Drops pan, and rushes out behind rock* R. 3 E.)

(*After a little,* MIKE'S *head is seen to rise above rocks.*)

MIKE (*in a hoarse whisper*). Joe! Joe!

JOE (*faintly*). Yiss, Moike, I'm here.

MIKE. Are yeez killed, Joe?

JOE. No, Moike, I'm alive; but I say, Moike?

MIKE. Yiss, Joe.

JOE. Did Tom Piper get the gold?

MIKE. Divil a bit, Joe. He dhramed a lie; but I say, Joe?

JOE. Yiss, Moike.

MIKE. Can yeez account for that terrible sound?

JOE (*coming from behind rock*). Yiss, Moike; it was a blasted owl. There he is now perched on that ould dead limb. (*Points off* C.)

MIKE (*coming down*). The ould satan. (*Looking up.*) Yiss, there he is, sure enough. Begorra! he loiked to have frightened me out ov me seven senses. I say, Joe?

JOE. Yiss, Moike.

MIKE. I belave the place is haunted.

JOE. I'm ov the same moind as yourself, Moike.

MIKE. I say, Joe.

JOE. Yiss, Moike.

MIKE. I kin shtand Matilda's tongue betther thin the outlandish noises ov this place. It's a duty we owe ould Ireland to save our lives, an' to do it we had betther lave at once.

Joe. Shall we lave the gold, Moike?

Mike. Divil take the gold. It's not for the loikes ov us to foind it, so come along. (*They pick up tools and start off* L. I E. *Noise outside; looking off.*) Thunder an' ounds! here comes those pros—pec—tus. Hide as quick as iver you can. (*Runs down stage. Hides tools behind rock, and climbs into tree* L. 2 E.)

Joe (*running around stage*). Where shall I hide? (*Throws tools off* R. 2 E.)

Mike. Tare an' ages! hide anywheres. If you kin do no betther, shtick your head into a hole loike a partridge, and kape shtill.

Joe (*looking at log*). Here's a hollow log. I'll crawl into that. (*Works himself into log. Music.*)

(*Enter* Mayhew *and* Blynn *with ax, pans, pickax, etc.*,
L. I E.)

Blynn (*throwing down tools and taking specimens from bag*). You, Mayhew, place these specimens among the rocks, and I will attend to the stream. Crosby will keep Bardwell back until we get the place well salted.

Mayhew (*taking specimens*). All right. By Jove! this is worse than the bogus mine swindle.

Blynn. Yes; but we are well paid for it. Two thousand dollars is not to be winked at. Crosby has paid us to do this job, and it remains with us to carry it out.

Mayhew. And if that girl don't interfere again, we will. She has made Bardwell suspicious already. By the way, how has she upset you so? I cannot account for it.

Blynn. The story is too long to repeat here. Suffice it to say, that a child of mine was stolen by gipsies, at an early age, and was never recovered. The shock killed my wife, after which I became reckless. This girl resembles that child. Such is my story in a nutshell. Now let us plant the gold. (Mayhew *goes up rocks, and* Blynn *down stage and off* L. U. E.)

Mike (*aside*). Begorra! there's something quare about this. Indayed! I niver knew they had to plant gold to make it grow; but perhaps it's the way they do it in this divilish America. (*In a hoarse whisper.*) I say, Joe!

Joe (*faintly*). Yiss, Moike.

Mike. Are yeez comfortable down there?

JOE. I'm moightly squazed, Moike. Kin I come out?

MIKE. No; kape shtill. The spalpeens are coming back.

BLYNN (*enters from* L. U. E., *and speaks to* MAYHEW, *who comes down rocks*). I can't help thinking how easily we fooled that Irishman. I knew at the time he would convey the news to Bardwell, and it seems he did at the first opportunity. (*Works in stream.*)

MIKE (*aside*). Thunder an' ounds!

MAYHEW. Yes; straight as a carrier pigeon. His shamming sleep was fortunate for us, for it paved the way for arousing the old man's cupidity. Well, what is wanted next?

BLYNN. Chop that log in two, and we will move one end up here for Bardwell a seat. We want him where he can watch us and not question our honesty.

MAYHEW. O yes! our honesty, ha! ha! ha! Well, here goes.

(MAYHEW *mounts log, facing audience. As he strikes the first blow,* JOE *is heard to shout.*)

JOE. Hould on there! Hould on there!

MAYHEW (*dropping ax and jumping from log*). What the devil!

BLYNN (*drawing revolver*). There's a man in the log.

MAYHEW. Shoot him, then. If you don't our scheme is ruined.

JOE. Hould on! hould on! don't shoot! I've a mither and tin children to support—

MIKE (*forgetting himself, and shouting*). Nine, Joe, nine. (*Recollecting himself; aside.*) The divil take me if I haven't cut off me own head.

BLYNN (*turning to tree*). What! another of them? Yes, and that pesky Irishman. Mayhew, attend to the log, while I bring that chap out of the tree.

(BLYNN *points revolver at* MIKE, *who scrambles down. MAYHEW points revolver at* JOE, *who draws back in out of sight. Music.*)

MIKE (*scrambling down*). I'm coming, your Rivirence. Don't be after shooting, your Highness. (*Landing on all fours.*) I'm wid you, your Majesty.

BLYNN. Well, what are you doing here?

MIKE (*rising to his feet and edging* R.). Prospecting, your Honor, if it may plaze your Highness. (*Bowing low.*)

BLYNN. Prospecting — eh! Well, just now your prospects are somewhat demoralized. Mayhew, bring that fellow out of the log.

JOE. Don't be after shooting and I'll come. I've a mither and tin children to support —

MIKE. It's only nine he has, your Honor, if it may plaze your Highness.

MAYHEW. Come! hurry up.

JOE (*emerging from log*). I'm nearly all out, sor. (*Rises and crosses to* MIKE, R. BLYNN *and* MAYHEW, L.)

BLYNN (*after a pause*). Well — what are we going to do with you?

MIKE. If it may plaze yer Highness, we will join the schame.

BLYNN. Then you have overheard our conversation?

MIKE. Shure I thried to stop up me ears, but they would kape open in spite ov me.

BLYNN (*aside to* MAYHEW). What shall we do with them?

MAYHEW. Offer them a tip to join us. It is our only hope.

BLYNN. I will try them. (*Aloud.*) Can you fellows keep a secret if you are paid for it?

MIKE. Begorra! I'm willing to thry.

JOE. I'm ov the same moind as Moike.

BLYNN. Well, you have overheard enough to know what is wanted of you. We will give you one hundred dollars apiece to assist us. Remember, though, if you prove treacherous, we will shoot you down like dogs. Are you with us or not?

MIKE. I'm wid you, sor — for a hundred dollars.

JOE. And I am wid Mike.

BLYNN. Mayhew, pay them the money.

MAYHEW (*paying them money*). Remember we shall keep an eye on you, and it is death to the one who shows the white feather.

MIKE. Niver yeez fear for me. (*Looking at money.*) Och! but won't Matilda grate me now wid a shmile on her face.

BLYNN. Now let them drag that log to the bank. Crosby and Bardwell are coming, and we must have things ready.

(MIKE *and* JOE *drag log up stage* L. C., *then cross to* R. I E, *as* BELLE, UNCLE NATHAN, *and* CROSBY *enter* L. I E. BLYNN *and* MAYHEW *remain* L. C.)

BELLE. Here we are, grandpa.

UNCLE N. (*looking around*). Lord bless ye, yes; an' things look jest as nat'ral as they did when I was a yengster, an' used ter play up there among the rocks. I didn't mistrust then there wus gold here, I — I guess I didn't.

CROSBY (*perceiving* MIKE *and* JOE, *he crosses to them and says savagely*). What are you here for — eh? Are you paid for this? (MAYHEW *crosses over and whispers in his ear*.). Oh! ah! (*Pleasantly.*) Prospecting — eh, Michael?

MIKE. Yiss, sor.

CROSBY. And you, Joseph.

JOE. I've found a hundred dollars, sor.

UNCLE N. (*overhearing last remark*). Er — er — what's that? You've been findin' gold too, Joseph?

MIKE (*confused and answering for* JOE). Yiss — yiss, your riverence; jhust a little. Joseph an' I found a little in the shtream.

BELLE. O my!

UNCLE N. You don't mean it! B-b-by John Rogers, you don't mean it! Let me see it — let me see it, Michael.

MIKE (*confused, and feeling in his pockets*). Yiss — yiss, your Rivirence. Yiss, sor, yiss. (*Aside.*) Bad luck to it! how can a man lie and spake the truth at the same toime?

BLYNN (*down* C.). Here are the samples. Examine them, Mr. Bardwell. (*Gives samples to* NATHAN.) They are the largest specimens found yet.

MIKE (*aside* R.). Begorra! I'm out ov that wid a clear conscience. I say, Joe?

JOE. Yiss, Moike.

MIKE. It's a mane shcrape we're in.

JOE. It is that, Moike.

BELLE (*looking at gold*). O dear! I thought gold was covered with letters and pictures like the piece I wear around my neck. Didn't you, grandpa Crosby?

CROSBY. No, no, child. (*Examining specimens.*)
Michael, did you find this in the stream?   •

MIKE. No—no, sor. (MAYHEW *nods to him.*) Yiss,
yiss, your Rivirence. Begorra! we scooped it up wid a pan.

UNCLE N. With a pan? Scooped it up with a pan?

MIKE. Yiss, your Rivirence, wid a pan; yiss, sor. We
have the pan here, sor. (JOE *and* MIKE *rush out after
pans and return.*) Here they are, sor.

UNCLE N. (*excited*). I want ter know! I want ter
know! B-b-by John Rogers! there must be gold here. If
our hired men can find it, Crosby, there must be gold here.

CROSBY. No doubt of it. I have been convinced of the
fact for some time. It is here, Nathan, waiting for us.

BLYNN. Now, Mr. Bardwell, if you will please be seated,
we will see what the sands of the stream will reveal. We
want to convince you that gold can be found in Rocky Run.

UNCLE N. (*seating himself on log*). Wa'all, I'm ready.
I—I—I'm ready ter see the gold.

BLYNN. Mayhew, you had better dig among the rocks.
The men and myself will work in the stream. Now to
business.

(MAYHEW *takes pick and ascends rocks* R. U. E. JOE, MIKE
and BLYNN *work in stream.* BELLE *stands* R. C. *watching them.* NATHAN *and* CROSBY L. C. BLYNN *drops
samples into pans unobserved.*)

UNCLE N. Crosby, look a-here a minit, I—I—I want
ter ask a question.

CROSBY. I am listening, Nathan.

UNCLE N. Now s'posin' there is gold here, an'—an' it
looks like it—it looks like it! what do you propose? Give
'em five thousand dollars an'—an' let 'em run off with it?

CROSBY. Far from it, Nathan. Everything shall be
legally arranged. They deposit with us bricks of gold; half
in your possession, and half in mine, as security for the
money we advance.

UNCLE N. So when I mortgage my farm, I—I hold
gold bricks as security.

CROSBY. Security against them, Nathan. Understand
me, security against them. If they decamp with the money,
we have the bricks of gold to offset it.

UNCLE N. Wa'all, s'posin' they don't decamp? S'posin'

they invest the money, an'—an' the gold don't hold out. What becomes of the bricks then?

CROSBY. Perfectly plain, Nathan. Upon completion of the works, we return the gold bricks, and release them from all responsibility. Our risk lies in the gold becoming exhausted. See?

UNCLE N. I see—I see, I'm beginnin' ter see. Those air bricks are security atween them an' ourselves. I—I kin understand that. Ter furnish my share o' the money, I must mortgage you my farm. I—I kin understand that, too. Now when they invest the money, them air bricks are ter be returned. Then, if the stream o' gold runs dry, the money is gone, the gold bricks are gone, an'—an' it's purty evident that the farm is gone, too.

CROSBY. Tut, tut, Nathan. The investment is secure. Trust me for that. There is gold here—pounds of it. We have seen it for ourselves. There is money in the scheme, Nathan, money.

UNCLE N. There may be, Crosby; but somethin' inardly whispers that—that I'd better keep out of it. I've been swindled afore; an' I ain't too old ter be swindled agin. Then Gipsy whispered some dark things yesterday. Things that—that apply purty strongly ter you, Crosby.

CROSBY (aside). Curses light on that minx! (Aloud.) Oh, the girl meant well. I admit the advisability of being careful. It is how I have made my money, eh, Nathan? Did I not feel implicit confidence in this scheme, I should withdraw myself. But there is gold here. I have investigated, and I know it. I'll carry you through, Nathan. I'll anchor you safely—trust me for it.

UNCLE N. I hope so, I hope so. I can't believe you would ruin me meaningly, Crosby, I can't believe it. We are too closely united for that. We have lived as neighbors for many years, an' though different in many respects, still, we have never quarreled. We have followed our children ter the altar, an' we have followed them ter the grave. We have mingled our tears together, an'—an' we are both left childless in our old age. Before us is Belle— the blossom that is left—near ter you as ter me, Crosby, an' the link that should bind us together. Now with this one lone flower atween us, an' the memory of our dead children fresh an' green in our minds, I — I can't believe you would work a scheme ter ruin me, I — I can't believe it.

(CROSBY *fidgets nervously while* NATHAN *is speaking, and finally turns away* L. MIKE *has turned pan of gravel on bank* R. C., *and is down on hands and knees examining it.* BELLE *is assisting him. As* NATHAN *ceases speaking,* MIKE *suddenly jumps up with specimen.*)

MIKE (*holding up specimen*). Come here! Ivery mither's son ov you come here! (*All rush around him.*) Will yeez look at this, now. Did yeez iver see the loikes?

BLYNN. Sure enough. Here is the largest nugget found yet. (*Taking sample and showing it to* NATHAN.) I told you, Bardwell, there was gold here. Gold in abundance.

UNCLE N. It looks like it! It looks like it!

BLYNN. Now let us examine our work. (JOE *and* BLYNN *get pans.*)

MAYHEW (*coming down from rocks and showing samples*). Well, Blynn, I have equalled our find of the other day. More gold to the quantity of ore by one half, and a sprinkling of silver besides.

BLYNN. Better and better. (*Holding up samples of gold.*) Here are two good specimens in mine. (*To* JOE.) Friend, how is it with you?

JOE. It's all gold, your Honor.

BLYNN (*laughing*). Not so good news as that. (*Picking out sample.*) And yet, you are not without a specimen. Your eyes are disordered, I fear.

JOE. Yiss, sor. Touch ov a waterfall, the docther said.

BLYNN. What!

JOE. Waterfall, sor, waterfall.

BLYNN (*laughing*). Waterfall? You mean "cataract," don't you?

JOE. It's all the same thing, sor.

CROSBY. Nathan, can we want any further proof? Have we not seen enough to convince us that we are rich men?

UNCLE N. I'm satisfied — I'm satisfied. Bring on your papers, an' — an' I'll sign 'em.

MIKE (*loudly*). Oh, the divil! (MAYHEW *turns upon him and shows revolver.* MIKE *claps hand to his face.*) bee stung me, sor.

BELLE. Grandma told you to be careful, you know.

UNCLE N. Oh, I'll be careful. I've seen the gold — the gold is here. Then agin, Belle, these men respect gray hairs, an' — an' they may have an old white-haired father themselves, ye see, an' rather than defraud an old man like as their father must be, they'ed die fust — they'ed die fust, Belle.

BELLE. But men who are wicked don't care sometimes.

UNCLE N. Ha! ha! ye see, gentlemen, little Belle stands up for her old grandad, Lord bless ye, I guess she does. Why, Belle, these men won't deceive me, they — they won't deceive me.

BELLE (*slowly, and looking into his face*). But if they should, grandpa?

UNCLE N. If they should? If they should? (*Fiercely.*) Why, if they should, Belle, I — I — I'd curse 'em. I'd haunt them with my grey hairs till the sod covered 'em. I'd call down upon 'em the judgment of Almighty God; an' He who judges every man accordin' ter the deeds done in the body, would mete out to them the punishment they deserved. I'd do this, Belle; an' that God who stands by those who serve Him, will uphold me. Bring on your papers, Crosby, I — I — I'll sign 'em.

(*While* NATHAN *is speaking*, JOE *and* MIKE *go* R. I E. CROSBY *stands near* L. I E. MAYHEW *seated on rock* R. *of* C. BLYNN, C. NATHAN *and* BELLE L. *of* C. *When* NATHAN *says*: "*Bring on your papers, etc.*," *no one moves.*)

UNCLE N. (*after a pause*). Bring on your papers, Crosby, I'll sign 'em. (*No one moves. Pause.* CROSBY *fidgets nervously.* NATHAN *turns to him.*) Is there that in the papers, Crosby, that makes you afeared of 'em?

CROSBY (*searching his pockets*). No — no; I was look-ing for them. (*Producing documents.*) Here is the note. Now, Mr. Blynn, bring on your agreement. Everything shall be square, Nathan. You, Mike and Joe, come forward as witnesses.

MIKE. Begorra! I'll not be a witness — (MAYHEW *shows revolver*) unless Joe will.

JOE (*seeing revolver*). I'll be witness, your Honor. (*They come forward. Stage slowly grows dark, and faint thunder heard in the distance.*)

CROSBY. Blynn, here is the money Nathan and I agree to furnish. (*Hands him sealed package; aside to* BLYNN.) You understand. (*Aloud.*) Now bring on the gold bricks. (BLYNN *takes gold bricks from bag and hands them to* CROSBY.) There! now arrange a place for Nathan to sign the papers.

UNCLE N. I have a place, Crosby, a — a place on which ter sign 'em.

CROSBY (*looking around*). I fail to see it, Nathan.

UNCLE N. (*placing his hand upon* BELLE'S *head*). Here — here is my tablet, gentlemen. (*All show surprise.*)

CROSBY. You — you mean —

UNCLE N. I mean, that it shall be innocence beneath those papers, an' a God ter witness 'em above, an' if evil is in them, may they burn the hearts of those who wrought 'em.

MIKE (*aside to* JOE, R., ˉ*as* CROSBY *prepares papers to sign*). I say, Joe.

JOE. Yiss, Moike.

MIKE. I wish that hundred dollars was in the bottom ov the say.

JOE. I'm ov the same moind as yourself, Moike.

(NATHAN *signs agreement. Position of characters.*)

UNCLE NATHAN.
BELLE.
BLYNN.
MAYHEW.   CROSBY.
MIKE.
JOE.

R.   L.

CROSBY (*after* NATHAN *has signed agreement*). Now let the witnesses sign.

MIKE (*coming forward*). I have an aversion to the pen (*Sees revolver*) — but I'll sign. (MIKE *and* JOE *sign, then fall back* R. I E.)

UNCLE N. Crosby, give me the note. (*Takes note.*) If, through any fault of yours, I lose my farm, may the good Lord judge you according to the deed. (*Music.* NATHAN *signs note. Witnesses sign. Lightning and thunder.* GIPSY *seen on the rocks above.*)

CROSBY (*taking the note and putting it into his pocket; aside.*) Ha! I have conquered at last.

GIPSY (*shouting*). Nathan Bardwell! (*All turn and look up at the rocks.*) Don't you sign those papers. I have found their trunk of samples. This is the gold mine of Rocky Run. (*Stands on edge of cliff, clinging by right hand, and holding small tin trunk aloft in her left. Picture. Chord.*) (*All exhibit great surprise.* UNCLE NATHAN *staggers back, and nearly falls.* BELLE *clings to him.* JOE *and* MIKE *cling to each other.* CROSBY *shakes his fist threateningly at* GIPSY. *Scene closes with TABLEAU.*)

SITUATIONS AT CLOSE.

(*Rocks.*)
GIPSY.

MAYHEW.
   BLYNN.   UNCLE NATHAN.
                   BELLE.

MIKE.
  JOE.   CROSBY.

R.   L.

ACT DROP.

(*One year supposed to have elapsed between Act II. and Act III.*)

ACT III.

SCENE I. — UNCLE NATHAN'S *dooryard as in Act I. and Act II. As curtain rises,* JOE *is discovered seated on block* L. C., *smoking.*

MIKE (*enters from* C.). Yeez are not working to-day, Joe.

JOE (*looking despondent*). No, Moike. I'm out ov a job now. I've worked here for fifteen years going on, and a betther place I've niver found; but they turn Bardwell out to-day, an' it laves me no place to lay me head.

MIKE. Begorra! Crosby turned me off long ago. Bad luck to him! he don't improve wid ould age, loike good whiskey; but grows sour, loike ould grapes. I say, Joe?

JOE. Yiss, Moike.

MIKE. We hould the saycret that would let Bardwell kape the farm.

JOE. Indade we do, Moike; and I've a moind to revale it. I darsen't do it, though.

MIKE. No more do I, Joe. Thim pros—pec—tus threatened to shoot us if we told, an' Crosby says he kin hang us, an' between the lot they hould us fast. Have yeez disposed ov that hundred dollars yet?

JOE. No, Moike; I've hidden it away. It's not the courage I have to shpend it.

MIKE. No more have I, Joe. Shure and I belave the stuff is counterfeit.

JOE (*looking up quickly*). Have you rasons for belaving that, Moike?

MIKE. I have that, Joe. I thried to pass a bill at the circus and they wouldn't take it. It's a moighty poor bill that won't pass at a show.

JOE. Faith, now you mention it, I thried the same thing. They called me a blackguard, and threatened to have me arrested. I hid them bills away.

MIKE. Yeez didn't have the courage to pass them, Joe.

JOE. No, Moike; they are bogus as the gold bricks an' the mine ov Rocky Run.

MIKE. Shure we are ov the same moind entoirly. I say, Joe?

JOE. Yiss, Moike.

MIKE. How does the ould gintleman feel over being ejected from the premises?

JOE. Don't mention it, Moike. It's not the courage I have to go inside the house. So I sit here and smoke, and think what a dirthy blackguard I am for kaping shtill over a matter ov self preservation.

MATILDA (*calling outside* C.). Michael! Mi-ch-a-e-l!

MIKE (*starting*). Holy St. Patrick! here comes Matilda. Shure I'd rather meet a conclave ov soldiers than Matilda on the war-path. I'll hide in the well, Joe, and when she comes, plaze lade her off the track.

JOE. I'll do me best, Moike; but if yeez are found out yeez must take the consequences. (MIKE *hides in well.*)

MATILDA (*outside*). Michael! Mich-a-e-l! (*Enters* C. *Takes* JOE *for* MIKE.) Oh, there you are, you brute. I've a good mind — (*Recognizes* JOE.) Ah, is that you, Joe? I thought you was that husband of mine. Have you seen him, Joe?

JOE. Not since the last toime, ma'am, no ma'am.

MATILDA (*leaning against well*). That is strange. I saw him coming directly toward the house. Have you been here all the morning?

JOE. Only when I've been away, ma'am. I've been here an' there — sometimes there, an' sometimes here.

MATILDA. Why, then you must have seen him.

JOE. I must, ma'am, if he was here, assuredly, ma'am.

MATILDA. Possibly he went into the house.

JOE. He moight, ma'am. There's a back door to the house, ma'am.

MATILDA. Well, let him go. He's not worth looking after, anyway. (*Looking at* JOE *coquettishly.*) Do you know, Joseph, if he resembled you, I should think a great deal more of him?

JOE (*quickly*). You moight, ma'am. Yiss, ma'am, av coorse, ma'am.

MATILDA. But he don't. He is the most insignificant specimen of a man I ever saw. He is shiftless, and boorish, and ugly, and never furnishes me with money. Ugh! I should like to hurl him into this well.

JOE (*growing nervous*). Av coorse, ma'am; yiss, ma'am.

MATILDA (*approaching* JOE *affectionately*). But you, Joseph, are just the man a woman would admire. You are so pleasant, you know, and considerate. I wonder you never think of getting married, Joseph?

JOE (*fidgeting nervously*). I'm too old, ma'am. I've a mither an' tin children to support —

MIKE (*in a hoarse whisper*). Nine, Joe, nine!

MATILDA (*starting*). Mercy! what was that?

JOE. Only the wind, ma'am. I've heard it before, ma'am.

MATILDA. Well, never mind. (*Places her hand lovingly upon his shoulder.* MIKE *seen peeking out of well.*) Do you know, Joseph, you would have been the man of my choice? I could love —

JOE (*moving uneasily*). They turn Bardwell out of the house to-day, ma'am. Crosby wid officers are coming —

MATILDA. Well, let them come, who cares. I have often wanted to talk with you, Joseph, and this is my first opportunity. You are so much superior to Mike that I cannot help loving you. (*Slipping her arm around his neck.*)

JOE (*partly turning around on block*). Bardwell's cow slipped over the ledge last night, an' broke her neck. It's trouble upon trouble that man has —

MATILDA. Joseph, listen to me. I'm married, I know; but I was led into it by not knowing my own mind. Had I thought of you then as much as now —

JOE (*speaking loudly*). A skunk killed tin chickens for Tom Lankins last week by climbing into the stable window. They knowed it was a skunk by the shmell.

MATILDA. Dear me; can't you listen to what I am saying? What do I care about skunks, and chickens, and dead cattle. Only give your consent, and I'll seek a divorce from Mike at once. (*Throwing her arms around him.*) Oh, Joseph! you must have me.

MIKE (*shouting excitedly*). Yeez kin have her, Joe! Yeez kin have her! (*Recollecting himself.*) Oh, the divil! (*Disappears.*)

MATILDA (*starting back with a scream*). Mercy! where is he? Mike has been watching us. O Joseph! support me, I'm fainting. (*Falls into his arms;* JOE *supports her awkwardly.*)

JOE (*shouting*). Moike! Moike! come here quick!
Come here! Matilda's having a fit.

MIKE (*down in well*). Have it out with her, Joe. I'll
not interfere. She's fit me more thin once. If yeez can't
conquer her, knock her on the head wid a brick.

MATILDA (*jumping up*). Oh, you brute! I'll teach you
to insult me like this. (*Rushes to well and looks in.* JOE
remains L. I E.) There you are — are you? Oh, I'll fix
you now. (*Takes bucket of water and pours part of it on to
him.*) Knock me on the head with a brick, will you?
(*Pours more water.*)

MIKE (*down in well*). Don't! don't! Matilda. I didn't
mane it! I didn't mane it, I tell ye.

MATILDA (*throwing water*). Knock me on the head
with a brick — eh? Don't you climb up, if you do, I'll rap you
with the bucket. Oh I've got you right where I want you.
(*Throwing water.*) Want to hit me with a brick, do you?

MIKE (*shouting*). Joe! Joe! take her away! For the
love of Heaven, take her away! It's drownding me she is
complaytely.

JOE (*approaching*). Matilda, yeez had betther —

MATILDA. Shut up! or I'll serve you the same way.
(JOSEPH *falls back.*) You deceived me. You led me into
this knowingly. (*To* MIKE.) Oh, you vile wretch! I've a
good mind to drown you.

GIPSY (*entering* C.). What are you looking at, Matilda;
your face in the well?

MATILDA. Yes; it's my face, every particle of it. Just
look at it; isn't it lovely?

GIPSY (*looking into well*). Why, Mike, for mercy's sake!
what are you doing down there?

MIKE. She's kaping me here, Gip. Take her away, an'
let me out ov this.

GIPSY. Oh, Matilda, let him come up.

MATILDA (*laughing*). Yes, I'll let him come up. I'll
just sprinkle him once more, though. (*Throws balance of
water into well.*) Ha! ha! ha! hit me on the head with a
brick again, won't you? (*Sets down bucket and starts off.*)
Well, good-bye. Wipe him down with a towel, Gipsy, he'll
need it. (*Goes off* C., *singing.*) Come, Michael! dear
Mich-a-e-l! come h-o-m-e.

GIPSY. She has gone, Mike, so now you can climb out. (MIKE *climbs out of well. He is wet, hair dishevelled, and looks badly used up.*) Ha! ha! you are a sorry sight, I must confess.

MIKE (*coming down front*). Niver has Michael O'Connor been used loike this since the day he was tilted into a mud puddle by Tim Rafferty's goat. Begorra! I'll aythur commit suicide, before night, or I'll join some regiment, an' die fighting the nagers.

GIPSY. No you won't, Michael. After you dry your clothes, and get over being frightened, you'll be livelier than ever. The trouble is you are void of manly courage.

JOE (L. I E.). You're roight, ma'am. He's not the spunk av a louse.

MIKE. Tare an' ages! where is your own courage, you spalpeen? Why didn't yeez drag Matilda from the well when I shouted to yeez?

JOE. Would a gintleman loike meself be afther touching a woman? It is more rispect I have for the gentler sex.

MIKE. Begorra! so have I (Aside.) when I can't help it.

BELLE (*appearing in doorway*). O Gipsy! I am so glad to see you. (*Runs to* GIPSY *and kisses her. Perceives* MIKE.) Why, what is the matter with Mike?

GIPSY (*laughing*). Oh, Mike has been on a little matter of exploration, that's all.

MIKE. Digging for gold, acushla.

JOE. Yiss; an' he found it in the well.

BELLE. Oh, Gipsy, will they turn grandpa out of the house to-day? He says he will never go only as they drag him out. I think grandpa Crosby is real mean, don't you?

GIPSY. His irregularities might be improved upon, I must confess. Where is Uncle Nathan; in the house?

BELLE. Yes; he heard your voice, and said he wanted to see you. He will be here in a minute. (*Looking toward house.*) Oh, he is coming now. (*Runs out to meet him, followed by* GIPSY.)

JOE. Mike, come to the barn. When Bardwell is around I feel moighty unazy in me moind.

MIKE. So do I, Joe. Since I took that hundred dollars, the wurld seems upside down; an' something whispers: "Michael! you're the greatest rogue on earth." Go on, Joe. (JOE *and* MIKE *exit* L. I E. ; *enter* UNCLE N.)

UNCLE N. (BELLE *and* GIPSY *assist him down steps. His face shows traces of weeping*). That's right! that's right, Belle; you'll help your old grandad, won't ye? Well, well, Gipsy, I'm glad ter see ye — right down glad ter see ye.

GIPSY. I knew you would be, Uncle Nathan, and that is why I came over. Let Belle and me assist you to a seat. (*They help him to bench near door.*)

UNCLE N. Yes, you may — you may, Gipsy. I'm rattled to-day, sorter off my pins, I guess; but I — I wanted ter see ye, Gipsy. (*Sits down.* BELLE R. *and* GIPSY L. *of him.*) There! that's right. I — I — I'm all right now. Yes, I wanted ter see ye, Gipsy. This may be the last time we shall meet under the old home roof, so I wanted ter see ye.

BELLE. Oh, grandpa! will they take you away from the old farm?

UNCLE N. Yes, Belle, yes. I couldn't meet the note, ye know, an' so the old farm must go. I've been notified, an' the time specified by law has expired, so now I must take the consequences.

GIPSY. Have you any place in view, Uncle Nathan?

UNCLE N. Only one, Gipsy; an' — an' I hate ter mention it. Ye see, when a man becames old, an' without any means of support, you know what comes next, Gipsy, you know what comes next.

GIPSY. Is it possible that you have got to go to the poor farm?

UNCLE N. It looks like it, Gipsy, it looks like it. Maria an' I have talked the matter all over, an' prayed ter the good Lord ter help us — an' I think he will, Gipsy, I think he will; but somehow, jest now, the way looks dark an' cloudy, an' it does seem as if the old farm must go. (*Wipes tears from his eyes.*)

BELLE. There, there, grandpa, don't cry, please don't. You've got Gipsy who loves you, and who comes to see you, and you've got grandma, and you've got Belle, too, you know, and we all love you.

UNCLE N. Lord bless ye! so ye do — so ye do, Belle. The Lord has been good ter me, that's a fact, an' I should not murmur. But when I think of them takin' the old farm, takin' it from me through ways I cannot explain, an' for things I never had, I can't help feeling angry, Belle, an' — an' wishin' things was different.

GIPSY. Father Crosby might give you the farm, and then be rich as a Jew. Oh, I should like to handle his money for a while, I'd make it jingle, don't you think I wouldn't.

UNCLE N. Crosby worships money, Gipsy, idolizes it as his God. But a day will come when he will wish he had worshiped some other God than mammon. He swore to have this farm years ago; an'—an' through fair means or foul he has got it; but it'll haunt him, Gipsy, it'll haunt him.

BELLE. Well, where you and grandma go, I shall go, if it is to Halifax.

UNCLE N. No, no, Belle. Crosby will take you to his own home, an' perhaps it is for the best.

BELLE. I won't go to grandpa Crosby's. I won't—I won't—I won't—

UNCLE N. You will have Gipsy with you, Belle.

BELLE (*throwing her arms around his neck*). Yes, but I can't leave you; you know I can't.

GIPSY. Wherever he goes, you shall see him, Belle. And he shall have a bed to sleep on to-night, if you and I, Belle, have to take mine on our shoulders and carry it to him.

UNCLE N. You—you would sacrifice much for my sake, both on ye; but sometimes, ye know, friendship can't save us when it would serve us most. I wus notified ter leave an' —an' I should have done it; but I couldn't, Gipsy, I—I— I couldn't. I started to take the old family portraits from the wall, them as have hung there through my fathers' day an' mine; but when I touched 'em, they—they seemed ter reproach me, an' so I left 'em alone. I'll let 'em hang there till they tear 'em down; an' I'll not cross that threshold until they take me up bodily an' bear me away. I'll not do it, I say. I love the old farm; an' that which I love I will protect, even at the peril of my life. (*Rises to his feet agitated.*)

BELLE. Oh, grandpa! where are you going?

UNCLE N. I—I—I'm going into the house, Belle. I'll protect it even as a lioness protects her young; an' if they want me, they must drag me out.

BELLE (*following him*). Grandma said you must not show resistance.

UNCLE N. (*in doorway*). I—I—I can't show much

resistance, Belle; but when it comes ter surrendering my farm, I'll never do it. Won't you come in, Gipsy?

GIPSY. No, Uncle Nathan. I want to free my mind, and in order to do it, I want all out doors. They will be here soon, and — (*looking off*) Here they come now.

UNCLE N. Wa'all, let 'em come. I'm ready for 'em — I — I'm ready for 'em. (*Exit into house.* BELLE *leans against side of house* R. GIPSY *crosses to well.*)

(CROSBY *and* SHERIFF *enter* C.)

CROSBY (*perceiving* GIPSY). Ha! you here? Why do I find you under foot everywhere I move?

GIPSY. Because I am a worm in your path; but don't you tread on me; if you do, I'll bite.

CROSBY. You will — eh? Mighty important you are getting of late. What are you doing here?

GIPSY. I am here to protect an old and decrepid man against the machinations of a man without principle or honor; and by that courage which I inherited from unknown parents, I'll do it.

CROSBY. Fine talk, this. Protect Bardwell, eh? How'll you do it?

GIPSY. With my tongue. I'll denounce you with my every breath. I'll hiss it in your face until I make life a burden to you.

CROSBY. This talk to me — me, your protector? You, whom I took as a beggarly brat and could discharge as the same? (*Starting toward her with hands clinched.*) I've a good mind —

GIPSY (*warns him off*). Touch me if you dare.

CROSBY (*starting back*). Ah-ha! threaten me, *eh? Have a care, girl, have a care; or not a cent of my money will you ever get. I'm not to be trifled with. Keep your mouth shut or I may strike you.

GIPSY. Ha! ha! ha! strike me, will you? (*Takes pistol from her pocket.*) Do you see that? Lay a finger upon me and you will find me a human tigress. I never expect your money. Neither do I want money that is obtained through fraud. (*Enter* JOE *and* MIKE L. 1 E., *and listen.*)

CROSBY. Fraud? You call this fraud, eh? I am performing a duty sanctioned by law.

GIPSY. It is a lie. If the law knew what I know it would denounce you as a swindler.

CROSBY (*startled*). What do you mean, girl?

GIPSY. I mean, that you talk in your sleep, and I have heard you. What you said has convinced me that you planned that whole gold scheme yourself.

CROSBY (*starting toward her*). What!

GIPSY (*pointing pistol*). Stand back! Come too near at your peril. I say, you concocted this plot to rob Uncle Nathan of his farm. Could I prove it I can tell you that you would never succeed.

CROSBY. Of course you can't prove it. What you talk is of your own fabrication. I am a victim of that gold scheme as well as Bardwell. I invested money for him. Because we were both victimized, and the gold bricks were bogus, am I to lose the whole? Out upon such nonsense! Sheriff, perform your duty.

GIPSY. Go on, old man. You may have invested money, but I doubt it. Turn Uncle Nathan and his wife into the street if you want to. Laugh at their tears, and gloat over their misery. Take the girl and abuse her as you have me until she learns to hate you. Do all this, and then retire, and sleep the sleep of innocence if you can. I have finished. (*Folds her arms and leans against well frame.*)

CROSBY. It's well that you have. I will settle with you at another time. Sheriff, do as I bade you. (SHERIFF *crosses to door and raps.* BELLE *crosses to* GIPSY.)

JOE (*aside to* MIKE). Do yeez talk in your slape, Moike?

MIKE. Divil a bit do I know, Joe. I niver laid awake to see. Begorra! if I did, I'd niver slape afther this without kaping one ear open to listen to meself.

JOE. No more would I, Moike.

MRS. B. (*opening door*). What is wanted?

SHERIFF (*bowing low*). Aw — weally, Mrs. Bardwell, I must take possession of this house in the name of the law. A sad duty, but weally necessary, don't you know.

MRS. B. (*coming down*). I shall offer no resistance.

CROSBY. I am sorry, Mrs. Bardwell, to be driven to this extreme.

MRS. B. Make no excuses, Mr. Crosby. Your own conscience is your guide. Bear with Nathan, however. He is excitable and cannot bear trouble as calmly as myself. I will sit down here if you please. (*Sits on bench.*)

CROSBY. Is Nathan in the house, Mrs. Bardwell.

MRS. B. He is. Deal gently with him, and if possible, persuade him to yield without resistance.

SHERIFF. Aw — no trouble, I assure you. I will not be fierce — weally, I could not, don't you know. (*Exit into house.*)

GIPSY (*to* CROSBY). Why don't you follow him. Are you afraid of Nathan?

CROSBY. Girl, what do you mean by such language ? (*Turning toward her.*) I've half a mind to wring your neck.

GIPSY. Well, why don't you do it? Won't you commence now? It will only conform with your actions toward Nathan.

(*Noise of furniture falling in house, after which,* SHERIFF *rushes out excitedly, and down* C.)

SHERIFF (*shouting*). Fly! fly! He's got a gun! he's got a gun!

UNCLE N. (*appearing with blunderbuss and calmly seating himself in doorway*). I — I — I'm ready ter be ejected, Crosby.

CROSBY. Bardwell, be careful. You are resisting an officer of the law.

MRS. B. Nathan, do submit quietly. Do let us go without making any trouble.

UNCLE N. Maria, this roof has sheltered me for seventy years goin' on, an' — an' for fifty years it has sheltered you. It is our home. Each spot is as familiar to our eyes as the sun which rises an' sets. Now, d'yer think I'm goin' ter desert the old place for strangers to desecrate? D'yer think it, Maria?

MRS. B. But you signed the note, Nathan, and must expect to suffer the consequences.

UNCLE N. I wus influenced — influenced, Maria. (*To* CROSBY.) I — I — I tell ye, Crosby, ye know more about that gold scheme than you reveal. The man who defrauds you, you follow as a hound follows a fox. Have you followed them gold seekers? H-h-have you ever tried ter bring 'em ter justice, Crosby?

CROSBY. Bardwell, I have no time for idle talk. If you refuse to submit willingly, we must resort to force. Sheriff, perform your duty.

SHERIFF. Aw—but, Mr. Crosby, he has a gun. A gun is a dangerous weapon. It is liable to go off, don't you know.

CROSBY. You are employed to take possession of these premises. Relieve him of that weapon.

SHERIFF. Aw — but, weally, I must decline. I couldn't do it, don't you know.

CROSBY. Do you refuse to act in the capacity of sheriff?

SHERIFF. Oh, no; but at present he holds the fort, don't you see. Weally, you must use diplomacy, don't you know.

CROSBY. You are a coward. (*To* MIKE.) Mike, you and Joe get possession of that gun, and I will give you twenty dollars.

MIKE. Begorra! I'll see ye hanged first. If yeez wants the gun yeez can go and get it.

JOE. And I am ov the same moind as Moike.

GIPSY. You can see where your friends are, father Crosby?

CROSBY (*excitedly*). Hold your tongue. I'll have that gun if I take it myself. Bardwell, what do you mean by this obstinacy.

UNCLE N. I am guarding my home against insult and robbery.

CROSBY. Robbery? Who is the robber? Did you not sign those papers? Did I not invest my money for you? Who is the robber — eh?

UNCLE N. I — I have my doubts about your investing that money, Crosby.

MIKE (*aside*). Begorra! so have I.

CROSBY. Bardwell, will you lay down that gun, or shall I take it from you?

MRS. B. Oh, Nathan, for my sake do not cause any trouble. I would rather die than have you commit an act that we should be sorry for.

UNCLE N. If he wants the gun he must take it, Maria; take it at his own risk.

CROSBY. And I'll assume that risk. Shoot me if you

dare. (*Music.* CROSBY *springs forward quickly and seizes gun before* BARDWELL *can raise it.. The women scream, and* BELLE *runs to* MRS. BARDWELL.)

SHERIFF (*running to* CROSBY'S *assistance*). I'm weally sorry to be so fierce, but it is weally necessary, don't you know. (*Helps* CROSBY *drag* NATHAN *down* C.)

GIPSY. Release him! (*Grasps* CROSBY *by shoulder and throws him over to* L. *Slaps* SHERIFF *in the face, who cries,* "*O Lord!*" *and runs toward house.* GIPSY *supports* U. NATHAN. *At same time* MIKE *and* JOE, *both frightened, keep each other back. Business.*)

CROSBY (*angrily*). Curse you! you hussy, you have gone one step too far. (*Starts forward.* MIKE *catches him by coat-tail and drags him back. Then whirls* JOE *around before* CROSBY *can see who caught him.*) Let me alone. (*Strikes back of him, then starts forward again.*)

GIPSY (*pointing pistol*). Don't you come too near. (CROSBY *stops.*) Your authority relates to the place and not to Nathan. Touch him again at your peril.

(GIPSY *stands* C., *with pistol pointed at* CROSBY, L. C. MRS. BARDWELL *supports* NATHAN, R. C. BELLE *beside her.* SHERIFF *in doorway.* MIKE *and* JOE, L. 1 E.)

SITUATIONS AT CLOSE.

BELLE.

MRS. BARDWELL.

UNCLE NATHAN.

(*Well.*)

GIPSY.

(*House.*)   SHERIFF.

CROSBY.   JOE.

MIKE.

R.   L.

TABLEAU CURTAIN.

SCENE II. — *Parlor in* SQUIRE CROSBY'S *house. Room well furnished. Archway* C. *Entrances* R. *and* L. *As curtain rises,* RICHARD BLYNN *enters* C. *Music.*

BLYNN (*approaching table* C.). Is no one at home, I wonder? No matter. I will content myself until some one arrives. (*Seats himself at table.*) This is the room where

Mayhew and myself were hired to work the scheme at Rocky
Run. Well, many changes have taken place since then.
(*Takes album from table and looks at it.*) Through them
all the face of this girl has ever stood out before me. It may
not prove that she is my daughter, and yet, stranger things
have often happened. (GIPSY *enters archway unperceived.*
BLYNN *looks steadily at picture in album.*) Heavens! here
is her picture before me now. (*Looks at it closely.*) How
lifelike it looks; and what a striking resemblance there is
between the features and those of my wife. Oh! should she
prove to be my child, my lost Irene. (*At mention of name,*
GIPSY *starts.*) God only knows the happiness that would
fill my heart. (*Rises to his feet and perceives* GIPSY.) Ah!

GIPSY (*turning to go*). I may be intruding. I will retire.

BLYNN. Stay. It is yourself I have come to see. Do
not leave me until I have spoken.

GIPSY. I have no desire to hold converse with one who
has been the instrument of ruining those I love.

BLYNN (*wincing*). Miss Crosby, at heart I may not be
the villain you imagine. That I have sinned, I cannot deny;
but that a man may sin, and afterwards repent, is not a
thing improbable.

GIPSY. If you refer to yourself, then undo what you
have done, and I will believe you. No person is truly
repentant who refuses to remedy an evil they have once
committed.

BLYNN. Miss Crosby, I am here for two purposes. To
remedy the evil you speak of, and to search for a long-lost
daughter. Will not this avowal command your attention for
a few moments?

GIPSY. Under the circumstances — yes. (*Advances to
table* L. BLYNN R.)

BLYNN. Thanks. I will be brief as possible. A moment
ago, I uttered a name which you must have overhead. Is it
not so?

GIPSY. It is, sir. The name was "Irene."

BLYNN. That name, Miss Crosby, belongs to one who,
if living, is the only tie which binds me to earth. Year after
year have I searched for her without avail. Discouraged
over my ill-luck — pardon me for my weakness — I fell into
bad habits. One folly led to another until I was hired to

work the bogus mine scheme. I met you, and you remember our conversation at that time.

GIPSY. That I bore a striking resemblance to your long-lost daughter.

BLYNN. Yes; and the resemblance was so strong that your face has haunted me ever since. The bare fact of your being a waif, found by the wayside, has strengthened this belief; but without some recollection on your part relating to your early life, how am I to ever prove that you are the daughter for whom I seek?

GIPSY. My knowledge of the past is extremely vague. At times, however, some incidents relating to my infancy seem to rise up before me, and I almost imagine them to be real. I frequently dream of a strange people, and of being in their possession. The name you mentioned bears a charm for me. It relates to something far away — something I cannot understand — something too indistinct to be real. When you uttered it, I started; my memory seemed to awaken; the past came up before me; and something, something I cannot fathom, connected that name with another.

BLYNN (*excited*). The other name; can you not remember it?

GIPSY. I could never recall it. At times, and frequently, too, it has trembled upon my lips, yet refused to be uttered. (*Thinking.*) It almost seems as if I could speak it now. (*Looking away abstractedly.*) A name so soft and tender, and so simple, that — that — Wait! does not the name begin with L?

BLYNN (*leaning toward her, excited*). Go on — go on. 'Tis the initial letter — the first letter of her name.

GIPSY (*thoughtfully*). L — L —

BLYNN. Go on. You must speak it. You —

GIPSY (*quickly*). Wait! you have spoken it. "U" is the next letter.

BLYNN. L — U?

GIPSY. Yes; Lulu Irene.

BLYNN. The name of my wife, and the one given to our daughter.

GIPSY. Have you any proof by which you can claim me as such?

BLYNN. Alas! no.

GIPSY. Is there no mark, or character?

BLYNN. Stop! there was a mark, in India ink, pricked into the arm near the wrist. It was a letter.

GIPSY (*excitedly*). And the letter?

BLYNN. Was L! the first initial of her name.

GIPSY (*showing mark*). Look at the letter.

BLYNN (*examining the letter*). The very same. I should know it among a thousand. Time has not erased it or caused it to fade. You are my daughter, my long-lost child, stolen by gypsies when but a babe, and over whose loss my wife went broken-hearted to the grave. Oh, my child, acknowledge me as your father! (*Starts to embrace her.*)

GIPSY (*motioning him back*). Wait! thankful though I am to find a father, I have found one whose soul is stained with crime. When I see that stain removed, then will Gipsy, or Lulu Irene, embrace you as a daughter.

BLYNN. You shall witness my repentance before the rising of another sun. When I left this place, one year ago, you was not forgotten. For the first time the money I had earned burned in my pockets. We went to the mines; that is, Mayhew and myself, and joined two others who had been successful in striking a claim. We worked together. One day an accident happened by which Mayhew and one other lost their lives. When dying, Mayhew mentioned your name, and it worked like magic upon the man who was spared. He grasped my arm and demanded to know where my friend had learned it.

GIPSY. And you told him?

BLYNN. Not then. When the last sod had covered the remains of our companions, and all had departed, we remained at the grave and told each other our life histories; and that miner and God alone know that Richard Blynn is a reformed man.

GIPSY. But the miner; what of him? For years I have been true to one who went to the mines, and whom I still love as devotedly as when he left me. Oh, tell me his name.

NED (*rushing in* C.). Ned Bardwell, son of Nathan Bardwell, a true scion of old New England. Gip, my girl, come to my arms.

GIPSY (*throwing herself into his arms*). Oh, Ned, have you come back?

NED. It looks like it, don't it ? Feel of me and see. Oh, I'm the real article, only in the rough. Shave me, and I shall come out as smooth as a horse chestnut. (*Kissing her.*) Gip, I could hug you all day; but I musn't. Blynn and myself have a work to perform, and must be about it. When it is completed, there will be more real happiness around here than this place has known for years. So now, Gip, to business first, and love afterwards. (*Releasing her.*) Where's Crosby?

GIPSY. Oh, Ned! he is cross as a bear.

NED. Well, trot him in and we will take it out of him. Oh; we know what has transpired to-day. How? Well, we witnessed it at a distance. Why didn't we interfere? Because we had other fish to fry first; and when they are fried — Never mind; you tell Crosby he is wanted.

GIPSY. All right, Ned. You make Squire Crosby reform, and reinstate Uncle Nathan in his old home, and I'll return your coat-tail, and turn a dozen hand-springs besides. That is, I would if I wasn't a girl. (*Runs out* L. I E.)

NED. So, Blynn, you have proven to your own satisfaction that Gipsy is your daughter.

BLYNN (R. C.). Yes, beyond a doubt.

NED. Well, Blynn, I love that girl myself. Now must I ask you, as her father, for her hand, or must I take her and elope?

BLYNN. Ned, you two are worthy of each other. I shall be pleased to see her united to so honorable a man.

NED. Look here, old boy, that's putting it on too thick. I'll try and deserve it, though, "Hang me if I don't!" as father used to say. Here they come.

(*Enter* GIPSY, BELLE *and* CROSBY L. I E.)

CROSBY. What are you here for — eh?

BLYNN. I have come to purchase the farm belonging to Nathan Bardwell.

CROSBY. Well, you can't do it. So now, go.

BLYNN. Can it not be purchased at double its value?

CROSBY. No. Cover it with bank bills and you can't have it. If that is all you want you have my answer. You can retire. (*Turns to exit.*)

BLYNN. Wait! if I cannot purchase the farm, I may take the liberty to demand it.

CROSBY (*quickly turning back*). What! demand the farm? You can't do it. I'll denounce you as a rascal.

BLYNN. And I'll own that I am one. More than this, I'll show you to be the greater one, and prove it.

CROSBY. You can't do it. You haven't a scratch to show a thing. Who's this man with you?

NED. I'm a lawyer. Be careful what you say, or it may go hard with you.

CROSBY. I'll say what I please. Leave the house, both of you.

BLYNN. Crosby, we will not waste words. You never invested a dollar on that Bardwell note excepting the two thousand paid us to work the gold mine scheme. That money I now return. Here it is. (*Throws money upon table.*) Now I command you to yield up that mortgage, and return Nathan Bardwell to his farm.

CROSBY. Ha! I'll never do it. What can you prove — eh? Show your papers — Bring on your proof.

BLYNN. Call them in. Time is precious.

NED (*goes* C., *and shouts*). Here you, Tom, Dick and Harry, come in here; you are wanted.

(*Enter* MIKE *and* JOE *from* C. *At sight of them* CROSBY *starts.*)

CROSBY (*agitated*). Ha! you here? Be careful what you do or say.

MIKE. We've turned states evidence, your Honor. Begorra! yeez had betther do the same thing.

JOE. And yeez will feel happier, loike meself —

MIKE. And rest swater at night; an' not have bad dhrames —

JOE. Or talk in your slape, and reveal your sacrets —

MIKE. And make people think you've got the tic-dol-er-roust.

BLYNN. You see, Crosby, the odds are against you. Yield up the farm peaceably, and not compel us to resort to the law.

CROSBY (*who has tottered back and sunk into a chair*). The whole world conspires against me. My friends, even, prove to be my worst enemies. Do I not know you as a villain? Can I not show you up as a swindler, a cheat and a fraud?

BLYNN. Can I not do the same with you? Yield up that farm, Crosby, and save trouble. I advise you to do it.

MIKE. As a gintleman, I'll advise the same thing.

JOE. As the protector ov tin children —

MIKE. Nine, Joe, nine.

CROSBY. I won't. I've schemed for years to get that farm, and I've got it. Now I'll hold it in spite of the devil.

NED. Crosby, look me in the face and see if you know me.

CROSBY. I should know you for a villain at first sight.

NED. Ah — yes. Thanks for the compliment. As the nature of my villainy may not be understood, I will explain. I am Ned Bardwell, son of Nathan Bardwell, and brother to the husband of your daughter. As a relative by marriage to your family, and a son protecting the rights of his father, I demand those papers.

CROSBY (*staring at* NED). You — you Ned Bardwell?

NED. I am. Answer quick, old man; will you give up that farm, or shall I resort to the law?

BLYNN. Crosby, choose the better course. I have sinned and repented. I have proven this girl to be my daughter. This knowledge, and my repentance, makes me a happy man. ' Take the same course, Crosby. Give Nathan back his farm, and we will keep all secrets, and believe me, you will retire to-night a happier man.

CROSBY (*meekly*). Gipsy your daughter? Not content with the farm, do you intend to rob me of her also?

GIPSY. Ned, you and the rest retire for a time. I would speak with father Crosby alone.

NED. All right Gip. I will leave you to accomplish what a regiment of soldiers would fail to do.

MIKE (*aside to* NED). Begorra! if she don't conquer him she has changed moightily since she conquered you.

(*They all retire* C.)

GIPSY (*kneeling at* CROSBY's *feet*). Father Crosby, you said a moment ago that the whole world conspired against you. Do you know the reason why?

CROSBY. Because the world is a fraud. People are fools. If a man schemes for money he is hated. I am hated. Were I to die to-day, who would mourn, who would feel for me a thrill of compassion?

GIPSY. Did you ever take into consideration that the fault might be your own?

CROSBY. No; I've no time to think. I've got money, and the people hate me for it. I've not a relative on earth but wishes me dead, that they may grasp it. But I'll cheat them — I'll cheat them.

GIPSY. Did I ever hate you, father Crosby, until you drove me to it?

CROSBY. You turned against me to-day. Even now you intend to desert me for a father you never knew, and who never so much as gave you parental shelter.

GIPSY. Have I said I was going to desert you?

CROSBY. No; but you show it in your actions. You conspire against me. They intend to steal back that farm, and you join them in that.

GIPSY. Father Crosby, which had you rather have me: a wicked, dissolute woman, full of intrigue and deceit, or one who is honest and upright, and above reproach? What would you do if I were the first?

CROSBY. Turn you out of the house.

GIPSY. Supposing I had said to you: "Let us rob Nathan Bardwell of his farm. No matter how, only that we may get it, and turn him into the street." Had I said this, what would you have thought of me?

CROSBY (uneasily). You are a woman. You would have been out of place.

GIPSY. What is honorable for a man to do, in the sight of God, is honorable for woman. You know, father Crosby, that you have defrauded Uncle Nathan. You know that it was right for me to resent it. Because I did so, you charge me with being your enemy.

CROSBY. Would you not anyway? Is it not natural for you to hate me?

GIPSY. No. Years ago I loved you with all the intensity of a child. Even down to the death of your wife you was kind to me. But during the past few years you have scarcely spoken a kind word. Every glance is a frown and every sentence a curse. If I do not love you it is because you won't let me.

BELLE (R. I E.). Once I tried to kiss you and you slapped my face. Grandpa Bardwell never did that.

GIPSY. I tell you, father Crosby, if you want to be respected, you must respect others. Friendship is made, not bought. Gold is a sordid metal and worth only its face value. It may furnish you comforts; but it can never smooth your dying pillow, or give you happiness in another world. One little act on your part would bring you both friendship and respect; and believe me, it would lead you to respect yourself.

CROSBY. It is well enough to talk. Talking is easy. Preaching is all right in its place. The next thing is to carry it out. How is it possible, eh?

GIPSY. By showing to the world that you intend to do right. Give Nathan back his farm. You have money enough without it.

CROSBY. What! give it up of my own free will? I could never do it, never.

GIPSY. Father Crosby, do you remember the words written in the family Bible by the hand of your wife before she died?

CROSBY. No; I have not opened the Bible for years.

GIPSY. Let me read them to you. (*Brings Bible from table, opens it, and places it across his lap. Kneels* R. *of him.* BELLE *remains* L.) Here are the words written on the page opposite the family record: "When I die, do not forget that I once lived, and loved you with a wife's devotion. For my sake, do not idolize wealth, but use it for good purposes, and to make others happy. Use your neighbors as you would have them use you, and love and protect the little waif in your charge. Serve your God faithfully, and meet me in that better world." Signed, "Your loving wife, Nellie." Have you followed her advice, father Crosby?

CROSBY (*in a broken voice*). Gipsy, you are awakening memories I would forget. I do not want to think of myself; when I do, it angers me. I have no love for myself. When I stop to think, I would forget myself—forget everything.

GIPSY. Then do those things which to dwell upon would give you pleasure. Close this day with an act that will elevate you in your own estimation. Join with us in making this a night of rejoicing. Will you not, father Crosby?

BELLE (*throwing her arms around his neck*). Oh, do;

and I'll love you like grandpa Bardwell. And — and I'll kiss you, too,

CROSBY. Could you love an old wretch as I am, child?

BELLE. Well, I could try. You would never let me, you know. Won't you let me love you now?

CROSBY (*disengaging her arm from his neck, he rises agitated and turns* L. I E. *Gipsy returns Bible to table*). If you can, child. (*Aside.*) Confusion! what did I say?

BELLE (*going to him*). And won't you love me, too, just as you did mamma years ago?

CROSBY (*aside*). Ha! she spoke of my daughter; and how like her she is herself. I had not thought of it before. (*Aloud.*) Yes, child; in fact, I think I have right along.

BELLE. Oh! I'm so glad; and won't you let grandpa Bardwell go back to his home, and like him, too?

CROSBY (*aside*). Ahem! that's asking considerable; but were my wife alive, I believe she would sanction it. (*Aloud.*) Yes, child, I'll do it! I'll do it! (*Aside.*) I feel better already.

BELLE. Oh! thank you. Grandpa Crosby, I'll kiss you now. (*Kisses him.* CROSBY *wipes his eyes with handkerchief.*

CROSBY (*aside*). I thought I was hardened — case-hardened; but I am not.

GIPSY (*approaching and placing her hand upon his shoulder*). Shall I call them in, father Crosby?

CROSBY. Have your own way, girl. (*Aside.*) I am sure my wife would sanction it. (GIPSY *goes* C.)

BELLE. I've got two grandpas to love now, and Uncle Ned. O dear! I wish he would shave his face. He almost frightened me. Didn't he you?

CROSBY. He did at first, child; but I hardly think he can, now. In fact, I am sure he can't.

BELLE. Well, Gipsy wasn't afraid of him, so I won't be. He don't know me; but when he comes in, I'm going right up and speak to him.

(*Enter* C., GIPSY, NED, BLYNN, MIKE *and* JOE.)

BELLE (*running up to* NED). Hello! Uncle Ned!

NED (*holding her off and looking at her*). Bless me! who are you?

BELLE. Oh, I'm Belle. Didn't you know that? I know you 'cause Gipsy told me. You like her, too, don't you?

You want to like grandpa Crosby, too; 'cause — 'cause he's better now.

NED (*taking her up and kissing her*). And you are my little niece. Well, well, I'm proud to know it. I am a friend to any man, little girl, who is square and honest.

MIKE. Begorra! so am I; and if it's reforming he is, I'll stick by him loike a nail to a plank.

JOE. I'm ov the same moind as Moike.

BLYNN. Crosby, if what I understand is true, I extend to you the right hand of fellowship. (*Offers hand.*)

CROSBY (*taking his hand*). And I accept it. I may be sorry; but time will tell. My memory has been awakened. I have no excuses to make — I hate excuses. I see things differently — that is all. Bardwell, here is that note. Destroy it. (*Gives up papers.*) There! a burden is off my mind already.

MIKE. Och! when I gave up that hundred dollars I felt just the same way.

JOE. I felt just the same as Moike.

GIPSY. Now I propose that we give Uncle Nathan a surprise to-night, and let it be an occasion for uniting us all together.

BLYNN. Do it, Crosby, and I'll help you. And if we are not happier than in plotting against him, then I'm no believer in repentance.

CROSBY. I am at your disposal.

NED. Don't start a new blast until I dispose of the old. (*Tears the mortgage in two.*) There! now go ahead.

BELLE. Wait! let me take them. (*Takes papers.*) Grandpa Bardwell signed those papers on my head, and they was a fraud. Everything that is a fraud should be served like this. (*Throws papers upon floor*, C., *and jumps upon them as curtain falls.*)

SITUATIONS AT CLOSE.

JOE.

MIKE. NED.

CROSBY.

BLYNN. BELLE. GIPSY.

TABLEAU CURTAIN.

SCENE III. — NATHAN BARDWELL'S *dooryard same as in other Acts. Household furniture piled up* R. C. *The motto " Welcome Home " in large letters, tastefully arranged, and so constructed as to be illuminated when necessary, is hung suspended* C. *Flowers, vines, etc., hung around the house in profusion.* CROSBY *and* BELLE *seated on bench* R. C. BLYNN *seated on doorstep.* NED *and* GIPSY *leaning against frame of well.* MIKE *and* JOE L. I E. *Time — evening. Curtain rises to music and song by company.*

MIKE (*after song is finished*). Shure do you know there is some moighty quare things in this wurld I don't quite understand ?

GIPSY. Why, Mike, I supposed you knew everything. If there is something you don't know, what is it ?

MIKE. Well, I don't understand why a turkey gobbler turns up his nose at a red shawl. Thin there is a four-footed baste as does the same thing. Have you an explanation, acushla?

GIPSY (*laughing*). Why, no; what made you think of that ?

MIKE. The soight of yourself rigged out in so much red finery. Do ye know, the thought struck me all ov a suddint, loike an inspiration?

JOE. I was struck wid a thought, jhust the same as Moike.

GIPSY. Well, what is your thought, Joe?

JOE. I don't understand why suckers brade faster than trout. Did yeez ever think ov that ? Be jabers! the good things ov this wourld are hard to get, while thim things that are poor swarm loike mosquitoes in spring. There's something quare about it.

NED. I should say so. People are queer, too. I knew of a man at the mines who grumbled because he had to dig through ten feet of solid silver before he struck gold. The time and labor wasted nigh ruined him.

BLYNN. Hold on, Ned. That is the first lie you have uttered since you returned.

MIKE. Begorra! I don't doubt him in the laste. He was only a quare man — loike the story. Now the quarest man I iver saw lived at the Cape. In order to fish he had to walk five miles into the counthry after bait; an' ivery toime he went, he carried a sap-yoke, two pails, an' a twinty-pound shtone to balance the twinty pounds ov bait on his way back. Now I call that a moighty quare proceeding.

GIPSY. Why didn't he get the stone where he got the bait? Then what balanced the stone on the way out?

MIKE. Och! that is the quare part ov it, acushla.

NED (*laughing*). Mike, I throw up the sponge. You can lie faster than I can. The strangest thing to me, however, is to see ourselves situated as we are at present. It almost places me back to childhood.

GIPSY. When you was the hector of the family. Well, let's change the subject. Are you sure Uncle Nathan will be here?

NED. Certainly. I sent a boy over to the poor-house to listen to their conversation, and he heard them plan to be here at nine o'clock. It is now after eight. They wanted to bid the old farm good-by, they said, when no one was around to molest them. Learning their plans saved making an excuse to draw them here. Do you know I can hardly wait to clasp that dear old mother to my heart?

BELLE. And I want to see grandma and grandpa Bardwell. Don't you, grandpa Crosby?

CROSBY. Well — ahem — yes; after I have seen them, I think I shall want to.

GIPSY. What do you intend to do now, Ned?

NED. We will go into the house, draw the curtains close, and keep watch. When they are well into the yard, we will laugh, and sing, and make them think the place is in the hands of strangers. Then, at last, we will open the door, give them a happy surprise, illuminate the letters, aad all make merry together.

GIPSY. It will be just splendid. Come! let us go in.

NED. Exactly! Blynn, open the way.

BLYNN. All right. (*Opens door and enters, followed by the others.*)

BELLE. Come, grandpa. (*They enter house.*)

MIKE. Joe, we are the tail end ov the heap. We bring in the rear.

JOE. Be jabers, we always did. (*They enter cottage.*)

(MATILDA *enters* C.)

MATILDA. If they think they can keep me out of their little game, let them try it. I found it all out if Mike didn't tell me. Oh, that deceitful man, not to tell me he was coming here! I'll pay him for it, though. (*Looking into window.*) Yes, they are in there. I can hear them if I can't see them; and Mike is with them. (*Goes and pounds on door.*) Let me in.

MIKE (*slightly opening door and looking out*). Who moight ye be?

MATILDA. Let me in, or you'll find out.

MIKE. Oh, the divil!

MATILDA (*pushing door open*). Let me in, I say. (*Enters house and closes door.*)

(*Music. Enter slowly,* UNCLE NATHAN *and* MARIA, C.)

UNCLE N. Here we are — here we are, Maria, creepin' up ter our old home like two thieves in the night. It don't seem right, it — it don't seem nat'ral, Maria.

MRS. B. We have this to comfort us, Nathan. We are not two thieves, but honest people. We come here to mourn, and not to steal. Let us be cheerful then, and it will make our burden much lighter to bear.

UNCLE N. You are right — you are right, as you always are; but it don't bring back the old home, it — it don't give it back to us, Maria.

MRS. B. No; but we can gaze at it here in the shadows, and that is better than nothing.

UNCLE N. (*coming down front with* MARIA). Indeed it is — indeed it is; but ter look at that door, an' know it is barred against us; that door which has opened ter my father's family an' mine; an' ter feel that I am responsible for it — it makes me curse the hand that signed those papers, an' wish I wus not a Bardwell.

MRS. B. O Nathan! don't say that. Men better versed in business than yourself have made mistakes; and many having once lost, and in spite of adversities, have started anew, and prospered, and been happy afterwards.

UNCLE N. Yes, yes; but they wasn't crippled; they — they wasn't incapable; they wasn't as old an' shattered as I am, Maria.

MRS. B. No; but if we, in our old age, with everything against us, could brave this great trouble, would it not be more to our credit? If I, as the weaker vessel, can do this, should you not assist me?

UNCLE N. You talk wisdom — you talk wisdom, Maria. You can reason better than I kin, an' with sounder judgment. I murmur too much, I admit it. Yes, yes; I've much ter be thankful for. Here is the old bench, Maria. Here it is just as we left it, an' — an' it will not refuse us a seat. (*They sit on bench looking around.*) It may be in my eyes, but things look different ter me somehow. Have you noticed it, Maria?

MRS. B. I see no change, Nathan, only in the furniture. You must look after that to-morrow.

UNCLE N. Yes; I must move it away. The old family portraits — can you see them, Maria? (*Rises and examines furniture.*)

MRS. B. (*assisting* NATHAN). I can hardly tell in the shadows; but I don't think they have been molested.

UNCLE N. Oh! but they will be — they will be. It seems hard; but they will be torn from the walls. They — they will be cast out, like us. (*Sound of laughter within.*) Hark! hark! (*Grasps* MRS. BARDWELL'S *arm excitedly.*) Did you hear that — did you hear that, Maria.

MRS. B. Yes, I heard it

UNCLE N. What was it? What did it sound like?

MRS. B. It sounds like laughter, Nathan.

UNCLE N. (*laughter repeated, mingled with singing*). There it is again! (*Excited.*) B-b-by John Rogers! I can't stand that! I can't stand that, Maria. (*Starting toward house.*)

MRS. B. (*catching hold of him*). Come back, Nathan. What would you do?

UNCLE N. I'm goin' in, Maria. They shan't revel in those rooms till I'm done with 'em. They shan't do it, I say.

MRS. B. Nathan, come back. You must come back. This place is not yours now. Come, let us depart.

UNCLE N. I can't. I — I — I can't do it, Maria. I'm glued ter the spot. Makin' merry in there is like makin' merry over a new-made grave, an' — an' I hate it. They have no hearts, no feelin', no sense of compassion, an' I'll tell 'em of it. I'll tell 'em of it. (*Starts forward again.*)

MRS. B. Nathan, you shall come back. (*Drags him back.*) Don't, for mercy sakes! spoil your good resolutions. If you love me, come away at once. Hark! they are singing. (*Both listen.*)

(*Song:* "*We won't go home till morning!*" *is heard. At close shouts and laughter.*)

UNCLE N. (*turning dejectedly away*). That's too much — too much. I — I kin stand anything; but that's too much. Come, Maria, I — I'll go. The last link that binds me to the old home is broken, an' — an' I am ready ter go. (*They move slowly down stage toward* C. *Soft music.*)

GIPSY (*opening door*). Uncle Nathan!

UNCLE N. (*turning and looking at* GIPSY *in amazement*). You — you among 'em, Gipsy? I — I —

GIPSY (*advancing*). Oh, Uncle Nathan —

UNCLE N. (*motioning her back with his cane*). Go back! go back! I — I — I don't want ye!

GIPSY (*laughing*). You don't understand, Uncle Nathan. We've got a happy surprise in store for you. Now guess what it is?

UNCLE N. (*still staring at her*). I — I — I —

MRS. B. (*grasping his arm*). Nathan, there is something back of this. Don't you see it?

UNCLE N. (*dubiously*). I — I don't see nuthin', Maria.

GIPSY (*laughing*). Don't you smell a mice, Uncle Nathan?

MIKE (*emerging from the house, followed by* JOE, BELLE, MATILDA, CROSBY *and* BLYNN). Arrah! Mr. Bardwell! it's meself has the honor to welcome yeez back to your old home with all the graces possible. (*Advances, makes grand bow, and crosses* L.)

JOE. An' it's meself what feels jhust the same as Moike; an' I'll hire to yeez for the same ould wages, an' begin work to-morrow. (*Follows example of* MIKE, *and crosses* L.)

(NATHAN *stares first at one and then the other without replying.*)

BELLE (*running up to him*). Oh, grandpa! don't look so funny. Don't you know what this means? Well, I'll tell you. Grandpa Crosby is good now. He's given you back the farm, and you must like him, you know, and —

UNCLE N. (*struggling to speak*). Er — er — wait! Given me back the farm, did ye say?

BELLE. Yes; and —

CROSBY (*advancing*). Bardwell, let me explain. In the past, we were farmers living side by side, and enjoying the friendship of each other.

UNCLE N. In the past, Crosby, in the past.

CROSBY. In time my daughter and your son were united in wedlock, thus forging a chain that should have linked us together in unity through life.

UNCLE N. But it didn't, Crosby, it didn't.

CROSBY. Our children died. Then, in an evil hour, my thirst for gain led me to forget my sense of honor, and I planned a scheme that left you ruined and adrift upon the world.

UNCLE N. I — I — I've realized it — sensibly realized it.

CROSBY (*forcibly*). Nathan Bardwell, memories long slumbering in my bosom have been suddenly awakened, To-night I am the reverse of the man you saw to-day. The change is sudden ; but no matter. He who tore this farm from you as ruthlessly as a savage would tear a child from its mother's arms, returns it to you to-night, free and unincumbered, and humbly asks your pardon.

BLYNN (*approaching*). And I, Richard Blynn, his accomplice, place myself in the same humble position.

UNCLE N. (*doubtingly*). You give back my farm — this house — give it all back ?

CROSBY. I do, Nathan. Already the mortgage is destroyed.

UNCLE N. I — I —

BELLE. You will forgive him, won't you?

UNCLE N. (*passing his hand across his forehead*). I — I must be dreaming, Belle.

GIPSY (R. C. *back*). No, Uncle Nathan, it is no dream. The farm is yours, just as they have said.

BELLE. And you will forgive them, won't you?

UNCLE N. Why, Belle, I — I don't quite understand it all ; but if this is real ; if — if they are not deceiving me, there is no forgiveness to ask. Lord bless ye ! they have it without asking. (CROSBY *and* BLYNN *shake hands with him.*)

MIKE (*shouting and throwing up his cap*). Hurrah ! hurrah ! for Nathan Bardwell, and — the Continental Congress.

JOE }
MIKE } (*together*). Hurrah! hurrah!

MATILDA (*crossing over from cottage to* L.). I can't see the use of making a fuss over nothing.

MRS. B. Nathan, the Lord never forgets his own. He has blessed us tenfold, and we should return Him thanks.

UNCLE N. We sartin should — we sartin should; but I don't quite realize it, Maria. What! the old farm ours once more — returned — given back to us? I — I — I don't quite see —

GIPSY (*laughing*). How things have so suddenly reversed. Well, this is a queer world, you know. To-morrow you shall have a full explanation. But tell me: arn't you happy to know that the old place is yours once more?

UNCLE N. Happy — happy, Gipsy? I — I guess I am. I can't express myself; I — I can't do it. I've jumped from darkness into sech bright light, that I'm dazzled — I — I'm dazzled, Gipsy.

GIPSY. Is there any other surprise that could render you more pleasure than this?

UNCLE N. No, Gipsy; no other surprise could ekal it. No other surprise under Heaven.

MRS. B. Hold, Nathan; would not the return of our boy give us greater delight?

UNCLE N. Maria, that boy is dead ter us. He deserted us — left us in our old age, an' is lost to us forever.

GIPSY. But if he should come back?

UNCLE N. He never will, Gipsy. He is either dead, or swallowed up in the vortex of the great world, an' — an' his parents are forgotten. He'll never come back, Gipsy.

GIPSY. But if he should, wouldn't you welcome him with gladness?

UNCLE N. Gladness — gladness, Gipsy? Lord bless ye! could anything ekal the pleasure of a lost child being returned ter his parents? Return me my boy, Gipsy, an' — an' I'll be the happiest man on earth.

GIPSY. Then prepare yourself for a second surprise; and you, too, Mrs. Bardwell: for Ned, your long-lost boy, is here.

UNCLE N. (*in great surprise*). Here?

NED (*rushing out from cottage. Chord*). Father! Mother!

MRS. B. (*throwing her arms around his neck*). Oh, Ned! my boy! my boy!

UNCLE N. (*staggers front and sinks down upon block*). Ned — here?

NED. Yes, father; Ned, your truant son, is home again to gladden your heart and comfort your old age.

UNCLE N. (*brokenly, and looking at him fixedly*). Ned!

NED. Father, you are in doubt; but a mother can tell her son under all circumstances. To-morrow, in a better light, and with my whiskers removed, you will recognize in me the boy who so foolishly deserted you.

MIKE. Oh! it's him, your Honor, shure enough.

MATILDA. Hold your tongue!

UNCLE N. Ned, my boy, returned? Are — are you doing this ter try me? Are you my boy, an' alive?

NED (*approaching his father and taking his hand*). Father, I'm the real article. There's no dross about me. I'm all here.

UNCLE N. (*rising to his feet and feeling him over*). Yes, yes, you are; you're no shadder! (*Excited.*) Maria! it's him! It's our boy! B-b-y John Rogers! its our boy!

MRS. B. (*approaching* NED). I knew him, Nathan.

BELLE. And he's been here all day.

UNCLE N. Maria, I'm young again; I — I — I'm put back twenty years in life. I could dance an' sing — (*Crosses to* CROSBY, R.) Crosby, give me your hand. I — I — I forgive ye. (*Grasping* BLYNN's *hand.*) Blynn, I — I — I forgive ye. I forgive everybody — everybody, I say. I love ye all! Lord bless ye! I forgive ye all!

GIPSY (*crossing to* BLYNN, R.). Now will I acknowledge you as my father, and salute you as such. (*Kisses him.*)

BELLE. And Belle will acknowledge her two grandpas and love one like the other. (*Takes their hands and stands between them,* C., BLYNN *and* GIPSY, R., MRS. BARDWELL *and* NED, R. C., *back.*)

CROSBY. And with God's blessing you shall have no reason to do otherwise.

GIPSY. Oh, Ned! I forgot. I have a present for you. You may need it. (*Takes coat-tail from her pocket and gives him.*)

NED. (*taking it and laughing*). Ha! ha! ha! the identical coat-tail, by Jove! Thank you, Gip. That was the worst tear I ever had, and you was the cause of it. For your sake I will keep it. Mike, illuminate the letters.

(MIKE *draws back screen, showing the motto " Welcome Home " illuminated.*)

UNCLE N.   Look! look! Maria; do you see that? (*Pointing to motto.*)

MRS. B.   I do, Nathan; and to me they are significant of two meanings.

UNCLE N.   They are — they are, Maria. They welcome us home ter the old farm again, an' — an' they welcome home our long-lost boy to his parents' arms.

GIPSY.   And closes the sequel to Placer Gold, or, how Uncle Nathan lost his farm.

BELLE.

UNCLE NATHAN.   CROSBY.

MRS. BARDWELL.

NED.

GIPSY.   JOE.

BLYNN.   MIKE.

CURTAIN.